Wild Runs the River

(

Center Point
Large Print

**This Large Print Book carries the
Seal of Approval of N.A.V.H.**

Wild Runs the River

GILES A. LUTZ

CENTER POINT LARGE PRINT
THORNDIKE, MAINE

This Center Point Large Print edition
is published in the year 2013 by arrangement with
Golden West Literary Agency.

The text of this Large Print edition is unabridged.
In other aspects, this book may vary
from the original edition.
Printed and bound by
www.printondemand-worldwide.com of Peterborough, England
Set in 16-point Times New Roman type.

ISBN: 978-1-62899-291-5

Library of Congress Cataloging-in-Publication Data

Lutz, Giles A.
Wild runs the river / Giles A. Lutz. — Center Point Large Print edition.
pages ; cm
ISBN 978-1-62899-291-5 (library binding)
1. Large type books. I. Title.
PS3562.U83W47 2013
813′.54—dc23
2013019092

This book is made entirely of chain-of-custody materials

Wild Runs the River

CHAPTER ONE

The buildings of Imperial swam up through the desert's heat haze. But desert distance was deceptive, and Mark Addison knew from practical experience how far he was from the town. The constant, shimmering glare distorted a man's vision until his eyes watered. It was still two hours until noon, and already the air was blisteringly hot.

Mark halted his horse to give it a rest though he had been making small demands on it. The only shade in the desolate waste was that cast by himself and the animal. He wiped his face and scowled at the sour, damp smell of the handkerchief. Ordinarily, the stretch of his good humor was endless, but today he was in an irascible mood. He needed a bath, and he was tired. He was two weeks behind schedule, and to a man with an orderly mind that was akin to treason. He had disobeyed orders, and his disobedience had cost money, something that was in scarce supply around here. The money wouldn't come out of his pocket, but it didn't lessen his self-criticism. As a shield against the pointing finger, he had the knowledge that he had completed a job well and thoroughly.

The gate was in at Hanlon's Heading. The volcanic nest of boulders at Pilot Knob had given him ideal anchorage for his barrier against the Colorado River. The gate made that bull of a river give up its destructive powers, and allowed through the water that would turn this desolate desert into an oasis.

He urged his horse forward. "Damn it. I did a good job." He smiled wryly at the sound of his voice. In this solitude, a man formed the habit of talking to himself.

He had exceeded his orders and specifications in building the gate. He used timbers far heavier than authority thought necessary, and the spillway to the Alamo barranca was big enough for three times the water it would ever be asked to carry. He knew that river as well as a man could, and he had both fear and respect for it.

Chaffey would scream about setting the gate sills all the way to the floor of the canal. Mark admitted that right now it seemed a useless expenditure of time and money, for the river level stood five feet higher outside the gate than the floor of the canal. But drought could drastically change the picture. And drought could happen even though Chaffey refused to take it into consideration. Mark had lowered the gate sill to the bottom of the canal to take advantage of every possible contingency. Then he put in flashboards to keep the river from pouring in too fast. Maybe Chaffey had a right to his screaming. This irrigation project was costing vast sums of money, and Chaffey was supplying it. It could be that Chaffey was beginning to feel a pinch.

Perspiration trickled across Mark's forehead to wind up stinging his eyes. He used the handkerchief again, holding his breath against its sourness.

He was tall, rawboned, with a natural leanness. His humorous gray eyes were set in a face burned as dark as a Mojave Indian's. He wasn't a handsome man, his face was all knobs and angles, but his teeth were excellent, startlingly white against his dark face. He had an infectious laugh and a virility that neither weariness nor weather weakened. He had a look of durability about him, the durability of well-tested whipcord. His hands were big, almost clumsy looking, but they could handle the delicate setting on a surveyor's transit with competence. In the main, he was content with his life. Give him a problem that was big enough, and all other irritants were swept away. He had a simple philosophy. No problem had every road closed to it. If it could not be attacked from one direction, there was always another.

His eyes glowed, as they always did when he thought of the dream. Someday, this sere and desolate waste would be green and flourishing. He could believe without weakening, for he had been wrestling with this problem for a long time now. But he pitied the emigrant families who came here expecting to find the irrigating of the Colorado Desert an accomplished fact. The high-flying phrases, in the brochures the Company sent out, made this desert sound like Eden. All a man had to do was to plant a seed, then jump aside to keep from getting knocked down by its popping out of the ground. If the brochures didn't actually lie, they lied by implication. They promised and inferred and carefully skirted reality. Mark had objected when he first saw them, and Clell Hodges had looked at him with that fierce, wild impatience.

"You believe it will all happen just as it says here, don't you?"

That had drawn reluctant agreement from Mark. But before he could marshal further argument, Hodges had asked, "Then what does a few more days, a few more weeks matter?"

Chaffey was the money man, Hodges the visionary behind this project, and two more diverse natures would never attempt to blend. Their constant bickering worried Mark, and he swore at the pettiness that motivated men. This dream of irrigating this desert was big, so big that it dazzled a man's imagination, yet it could be pulled down by the smallness of human nature.

Hodges' spirit always ran ahead of the necessary plodding pace of his body. He trampled roughshod over every obstacle, animate or inanimate. It was a constant irritant to other men.

Mark understood and forgave him, though he had known his share of raw scrapes that Hodges had inflicted.

He shook his head both in anger and regret. Hodges was an engineer, not a businessman, but he couldn't stand to see any of the credit for this project go to anybody else. So he tried to handle all phases of it and did badly with every one.

One thing was certain. The water company Hodges had set up to supply water to the landholders was so far behind its schedule Mark doubted it would ever catch up. The water was ready to be let into the valley. But the grid of distribution ditches wasn't completed. Hodges was purposely delaying them for some unknown reason. Family after family threw the same question at Mark: When will the water be here? He always got those questions for Hodges was never around to answer them. No matter how much he squirmed and ducked and evaded, he had to give them some kind of a reply. He never told them an outright lie, but he had come perilously close to it. He knew how those families were suffering. The Lorelei promises of the brochures had drawn them from all over the United States. They lived in heat and flying sand that could scour the enamel off a pan. They carried water for miles to merely exist. But worse was watching the steady shrinking of their money, money earmarked for seed and necessary equipment, and it was being spent for living. Mark understood the naked fear in their eyes.

The grumbling had already started. He saw it in the faces of men clustered in town as they discussed another hopeless day. Damn Clell, he thought with an unusual judging. Why wasn't he content to handle the engineering and let Chaffey handle the financing?

He squinted at the buildings ahead of him. The wavering was diminishing in their outlines.

If he ever grew too impatient with their progress, all he had to do was to recall Imperial's first tent. And that really hadn't been too long ago. Chaffey had hung the fanciful name Imperial Valley on this desert, and the town took its name from that. It was beginning to assume a look of permanence. Its frame buildings were raw and crude but far better than the first tents and shanties. It was growing like a mushroom. A half-dozen brick buildings were under construction, and the stage now made a bi-weekly run to Flowing Well, the only outlet to the outside world. And all that had been done on the promise of water. Imperial would literally explode when water actually reached it.

He pulled up before Grat Theobold's livery stable. The old man was asleep in a tilted-back chair, his hat pulled low over his eyes. It would be hard to call his age. He looked as wrinkled and dried as the last apple that had been forgotten on a tree, but his eyes had lost none of their alertness. When business was slack, Theobold grabbed a dozen naps like this a day, moving each time the sun touched him.

Mark swung down and walked to Theobold's chair. "I wonder how hard a kick it would take to send that chair over."

The fluttering of Theobold's lips stopped. "You try it. And I'd have to run a pitchfork through." He let the chair legs down with a bang. "Don't give yourself any credit. You didn't sneak up on anybody."

"I could've swore I did."

Theobold grinned. He liked Mark. Mark never abused a horse, he never brought one in all lathered up and hurting. Theobold had been here since the founding of the town. He had the inquisitiveness of the aged, and an uninhibited manner in satisfying it. So far, Imperial had no newspaper. It didn't need one, not as long as Theobold was around. He asked no hand of anybody. He ran a clean stable, and it would take a far greater rush of business than he had to make those spry, old legs falter.

Mark handed over the reins. "Take good care of him."

Theobold snorted at the unnecessary order. He led the animal into the shadowed runway, talking to it in a low voice. Mark smiled as he listened.

Theobold had a higher opinion of animals than he did of humans.

Mark moved to the gunny bag-wrapped water cooler. By keeping the bag soaked Theobold got some cooling through evaporation. He filled a dipperful. It was cooler than the tepid stuff in his canteen, but it had the same brackish taste.

Theobold came back as Mark drew another dipperful. "I've forgotten what cold, sweet water tastes like. Do you think water will ever get here?"

"Don't you start on me, Grat."

"Nobody can catch Hodges to ask him."

It was justified, but Mark felt irritated at the criticism. "If Clell stopped to answer every fool question thrown at him, he'd never get anything done."

"You stop to answer them."

"Maybe I haven't as much on my mind." Mark wanted to cut this short before it built up into an argument.

Theobold grinned maliciously. "When you can't answer, duck."

Mark was stung into giving more information than he intended. "It'll be here quicker than you think. The gate's in at Hanlon's. Sixty-five miles of the Alamo have been cleared, its bed leveled, and its banks raised. The irrigation ditches won't take long." He thought of the months of work behind that effort, the tons of lumber and tons of hay that had been bought and consumed. Large storage basins were completed and ready. Water was closer than anybody realized. But this last waiting was the hardest of all.

Theobold drew a quick breath. "Maybe that'll quiet us belly achers for a while, huh?" He shook his head in sympathy. "You're carrying too much of the load, Mark."

Mark sprang to quick defense of Hodges. "Without Clell pushing this through, this would still be a wide-open, empty space on the desert."

Theobold's face was set for argument. "Don't expect a man to see another's troubles. His head is too full of his own. I've been hearing more talk than ever this past week."

Mark didn't doubt it. And it wouldn't be still until flowing water washed it away. He walked to the mouth of the runway with the old man. "Have you seen Clell?" He wanted to report the finishing of the head gates and the ignoring of Chaffey's instructions. Even if Hodges disapproved, his dislike of Chaffey would swing him to Mark's side.

"Saw him early this morning. Not since. He runs in and out of here like his tail's on fire. Chaffey's in town."

Mark didn't want to see him, at least not first. He started to say something, and a voice from across the street interrupted him.

"Hey you," Hoyt Larkson bellowed. "Come over here. I want to talk to you."

15

The order had the rasp of a file.

Theobold's eyes burned with bright interest. "Didn't you hear him? There's your chief grumbler. All he does is hang around town and belly ache."

Larkson had Mahaffey and Adams with him. Mark's eyes narrowed as he watched them cross the street. All of them were farmers. It showed in their rough, sweat-stained clothing, in the clumsy, heavy shoes, and in their work-gnarled hands. These were men who had to have those hands filled with the soil, and they didn't know how to cope with their emptiness. They filled the idle time with useless talk and built up resentments. Mark understood, but it didn't make it any easier to bear.

Larkson was a big, beefy man with an awesome span of shoulders. Mark couldn't remember seeing him clean-shaven. He had small, suspicious eyes under beetling brows, and an aggressive way of talk and manner.

Mahaffey and Adams were cast in smaller molds with lean, wiry bodies. Perhaps size had something to do with it, but they followed Larkson's lead. Left alone, they might have been decent enough, but now, the same truculence was in their faces.

For a moment, Mark thought Larkson was going to walk through him, and he didn't budge. He had taken just about as much as he could stand from this man.

Larkson stopped close enough so that the fan of his breath reached Mark. It reeked of whisky, and that wouldn't make him any more amenable to reason.

The scowl deepened on Larkson's face. "Didn't you hear me?"

"The whole town heard you." Mark heard Theobold's quickened breathing at his side.

"Maybe you've got a reason not to want to talk to me."

Mark's eyes burned. A runaway recklessness was building up in him. He had placated this man all he intended. He was taking no more abuse of any kind from him. "Can't you say it plainer than that?"

Larkson's face flamed. "I've never been able to pin any of you engineers down before. All you give me is lies and soft talk. Now by God, you're going to answer me. I want to know when we'll get our water."

"If that's all you want, that's easy. When it gets here."

There was a smothered chuckle from Theobold.

Larkson's face burned bright. "Don't get smart with me. I got rights. I paid big money for my water stock, and I ain't seen a drop. You know what I think?"

"I don't give a damn what you think." The recklessness had full charge and was pushing Mark hard.

Larkson's jaw sagged at the unfamiliar bluntness. He stole a covert glance at Mahaffey and Adams. They stared back with challenge in their eyes.

Larkson's voice went up a notch. "I'll tell you what I think. I think somebody is putting money in their pockets. Somebody is getting rich off of us settlers, and you think we're too dumb not to know it."

The cords in Mark's neck stood out like small, rigid cables. He was losing control fast. He had been accused of a lot of things in his life but not of outright thieving. He dug in his fingers for one last grip.

"Let me make some things plain to you, Larkson. You paid eight dollars and seventy-five cents a share for your stock. But only a dollar of that was cash. You pay the rest in seven years. You paid a hundred and sixty dollars cash. And that's the big money you're talking about."

Larkson blinked. He reacted slowly when somebody threw figures at him. He searched and found a telling point. "There's more than me. How about Mahaffey and Adams? How about all the others?"

"If you want to know how your money is being spent, ride out to the Colorado River. Look at the work that's been finished and then tell me how much you think somebody is stealing."

Adams and Mahaffey exchanged uneasy

glances. Addison sounded damned sure of himself.

Larkson was a stubborn man. Once an idea lodged in his mind, it took strong roots. "That don't satisfy me. That don't—"

"I told you I didn't give a damn about what you think. Now get out of my way." Mark swept out an arm and shoved Larkson back.

He strode by him and heard Theobold's warning. He turned his head just in time to catch Larkson's fist on his cheekbone. It was a glancing blow, but it still spun and knocked him back into a wall of the runway. The ringing in his head told him how much power it had.

He hung there, needing the wall's support while he shook his head, trying to clear it. He had a hazy impression of Mahaffey's and Adams's open-mouthed expressions, and Theobold was watching him anxiously. Theobold needn't have worried. Mark had no intention of letting this stop here.

Larkson's teeth showed. "Maybe that'll teach you some manners."

He was a stupid man. He should have followed up that blow. Instead, he let Mark recover. He had the advantage of the first blow and of forty pounds of weight, and it wasn't going to be enough.

"Why no, Larkson. It didn't teach me that." It did teach him caution and respect for the authority in that meaty fist. It taught him not to get hit with it again, if he could avoid it.

He came off the wall fast. He couldn't gamble that Larkson lacked skill and mobility. He wouldn't go straight in and trade blows with the man, at least until he had worn him down.

He had been on the Michigan University boxing team as a senior, and he used what skill he had acquired. He feinted Larkson into a lead, countered and came in over it with a stinging left hand. It left a reddening bruise below Larkson's right eye and pulled a grunt from him.

He shuffled flat-footed at Mark, and a constant stream of oaths poured from him.

He gave Mark all the incentive he needed. He wanted to hurt this man badly now.

He slipped in and out, chopping the cutting blows into Larkson's face, and the toll began to mount. Larkson bled from several cuts, and his left eye was closing. He swung with ponderous futility, and he was panting like an exhausted dog.

He stopped his shuffling, and his face was baffled. "Stand still and fight."

Mark's shirt clung wetly to his back, and he felt the sweat trickling down his sides. His breathing had quickened, but he wasn't in distress yet.

The sight of that bleeding and bruised face wiped some of the wild anger away. He didn't like the man any better, but he could understand the frustrations that motivated him.

"Have you had enough, Larkson?" He'd give the man a chance to stop this.

Larkson's face looked uncertain. "Why, I guess so." His hands dropped to his sides.

Mark moved nearer him, and his hands were open. "Then we'll forget—"

He never got a chance to finish. He wouldn't have believed that much agility was left in Larkson. Larkson launched himself in a dive, and his head was a battering ram catching Mark in the stomach. Mark cursed himself for his stupidity even as his breath exploded from his lips. Larkson's momentum slammed Mark into a wall, and the power of his body tried to drive Mark through it.

He slid down the wall, and Larkson landed on top of him. It left him sick and stunned, and for several moments all he could do was to try and protect himself. If Larkson hadn't been over-eager, he could have finished it his way. His fists slammed at Mark, rocking his head back and forth, and weakly raised arms couldn't save him all of the punishment. Nausea filled him from Larkson's jolt in the belly, and the blows were scattering his senses.

Adams and Mahaffey danced around, whooping their delight, and the sound stirred Mark's anger afresh. This fight had been all his way until he had been criminally careless, and the self-blame and fury gave him a weak spurt of strength. He lifted a shoulder as though trying to roll to the left, and Larkson overcompensated, trying to hold him flat on his back. Mark put all of his effort into rolling to his right. Larkson's knee lifted and slid across him, and he made a wild grab at Mark. The splayed fingers hooked into his shirt, and the material gave, letting the nails draw fiery tracks across his chest.

But he was free of the crushing weight, and he kept rolling. He heard Larkson's hands and knees slapping at the earthen floor, as he scrambled after him, and the sound gave him speed. If Larkson pinned him again, he wouldn't get up.

He rolled half the length of the runway before he attempted to get his feet under him. At that, he didn't have too much margin. Larkson was a yard from him when he finally stood.

He shook his head to clear it, as Larkson straightened from his knees. "All right, you wanted it this way."

He kicked at the rising chin, and his boot scraped along the jaw line. It still had enough force to scrape the skin from Larkson's jaw and put him on his back. His eyes were glassy, and he made feeble, pawing motions with his hands. Mark was tempted to kick him again but instead used his fist. He had learned no blow like this on the boxing team. It was a roundhouse, low-swinging blow that swooshed by his ankle and landed flush on Larkson's chin.

Larkson's eyes rolled up into his head. He jerked convulsively and was still.

It wasn't enough to satisfy the anger that pumped through Mark. He glared at Adams and Mahaffey. "Come on, come on. There's enough left for you."

They stared from him to Larkson, then retreated a step. It was a more eloquent denial of his offer than any words.

A hand touched his shoulder, and he whirled, a fist cocked.

Theobold backed, and there was real alarm in his voice. "Hey, it's Grat."

Mark grinned and regretted it. The movement told him his lips were split. He touched a hand to them and found they were bleeding. He stared at the bloodstained fingers.

"That was a damned fool stunt. Letting him get in on you like that."

"I thought he was beaten." The less movement Mark made with his mouth, the less painful it was.

"He's beat now. Maybe even you can learn to tell the difference of what you think and what actually is."

Mark remembered not to grin. His shirt hung from him in two parts. He wanted some ointment to ease the stinging scratches on his chest. "I'm going down to Charley's and get cleaned up."

Theobold took an indignant breath. "When are

you going to tell Larkson and all the others to ask their questions of Hodges?"

"Clell pays me to do a job. I'm doing it."

Theobold's sigh had a degree of hopelessness in it.

As Mark moved toward the entrance, he heard Theobold yell, "Get this hulk out of here."

CHAPTER TWO

The fight hadn't drawn as much attention as Mark feared. A half-dozen people were clustered at the stable's entrance, and John Deeder asked, "What was it all about, Mark?"

"Just a personal argument." He moved on before more questions could be thrown at him. Deeder was a farmer, too, and Mark speculated on which side the man's sympathies lay.

He hurried down the street to Charley Ross's store, wanting to pull as little notice to himself as he could.

The sign hanging from the front of the store read STORE, in big block letters. Beneath it was CHARLEY ROSS, PROP., then two banks of words enumerating some of the items Ross sold. A man could buy feed, lumber, groceries, and drinking water. If he was truly optimistic, he could set in his supply of seed and scrapers and plows. He could rent a team and purchase drugs and remedies for relief of man and beast. Ross also ran the post office and sold water stock.

Ross was waiting on a woman customer, and Mark turned his back to her, pretending interest in a bag of alfalfa seed.

The woman's voice was indignant. "I swear, Charley Ross. Your prices get more outrageous every day."

"I'm making ten cents on that pan, Mrs. Heffner. I'm not getting rich."

"You're closer to it than we are."

Mark heard the outraged swish of her skirts as she moved out of the store. He kept his face averted. "Charley, if you'd quit trying to gouge your customers—" He waited for the explosion he knew would follow.

"Goddamn it, Mark. You know—"

Mark turned, and Ross's words broke off with a gasp. "Who chewed you up and spit you out?"

"Larkson. He questioned how the Company was spending all the money it gets from its customers. He made it personal."

Ross's eyes gleamed. "Did you whip him?" He was a little man with a balding head that he protected tenderly from the sun. The first thing he put on in the morning was his hat, and it was the last thing he took off at night. His face was nut brown, and it was startling to see all that expanse of white skin when he removed his hat. He had come into this desert at about the same time as Hodges and Mark, and he had seen the need of a store. He had set out his first meager supplies in the shade of the ramada at Blue Lake, and by the time they had moved here he was successful enough to build one of the first permanent establishments. Mark lived in a room in the rear of the store, paying a nominal rent for it. He had an attachment for this man, and he supposed he knew him as well as anybody could. But there were gaps in Ross's life he didn't know about, and Ross guarded them with a dogged secretness. Mark often had the impression that Ross was a lonely man, but Ross never did anything about it except hurt.

Mark touched his mouth. "I almost didn't. I made a stupid mistake and gave him a second chance."

Ross walked toward the back of the store. "Come on back here and let me clean you up."

Mark followed him, feeling the clamoring voices of the bruises and cuts. He hadn't realized until now just how much damage he had taken.

He took off the ruined shirt. "That's a new one. I haven't worn it more than a couple of times."

The water stung against his bare chest. Ross was as gentle as he could be. "He claws as good as a woman."

"He made a wild grab trying to hold me down."

"Clell should have to take complaints like this."

Mark put sharp eyes on him. That was the

second time today that he had heard something like this. It wasn't like Ross. The waiting was putting a strain on him, too. "He's doing everything he can."

"Is he?" Heated words trembled on Ross's lips, but he managed to hold them. "I guess he is—as he sees it. But everybody's disposition would improve a hundred percent, if water ever got here." He sponged the blood from Mark's face.

"Charley, the gate's in at Hanlon's." That should lift Ross's spirits.

"If the ditches were finished, the water would be here in the matter of a few days, wouldn't it?"

Ross knew it would. Mark wondered at this line of questioning.

"Mark, has Clell been dragging his feet?"

The direct question angered Mark. "Ask him. I haven't been working on the ditches." His frown deepened. "What makes you ask that, Charley?"

Ross made a helpless gesture. "You know the way Chaffey and Clell feel about each other."

Mark gave him no help at all. "No, tell me."

Ross showed a burst of anger. "Damnit, Mark. Do you know how rough it is on these people?"

Mark let up on him. "I know, Charley. I'm doing everything I can about it."

Ross refused to let go of his anger. "Somebody ought to do something."

Mark agreed with that. Maybe the gate's completion would be the spur. "Is Clell in town?"

"He's been in here a half-dozen times today asking if you've come in. He told me to tell you the minute you get here to get over to the hotel."

Mark bristled at the pre-emptory order. But that was Clell's way. But this was one order he didn't intend breaking his butt to carry out.

"I'm beat. I'm going to lie down first." He was entitled to that. He moved his face experimentally. Ross's cleansing seemed to have taken some of the stiffness out of it, but it was still sore.

Ross drew a cup of water from the cooler, and Mark drank thirstily. The fight had worn out that drink he had had at Theobold's.

He ran his tongue around the inside of his teeth and grimaced. It was still a long way from being good water. Hauling it long distances gave it a brackishness that couldn't be removed.

He caught Ross's judging eyes on him. "I'm not complaining. It's still better than the water we had at Blue Lake."

Ross almost smiled. "I remember it. And I remember all those schools of Colorado salmon that the prior spring's flood left. When the lake started going down, those dying fish beat the surface to foam. And my God, the pelicans that came in from Mexico to eat them. Their droppings almost turned that lake to solid matter." He looked as though he wanted to spit to get the memory of the taste out of his mouth.

Mark grinned. They were in rapport again with

28

an experience mutually shared. "We took shotguns and waded out to drive the birds away so we could dip up water. And wasn't it beautiful stuff? We strained the larger solids through cotton sacks, then poured the remaining water through a long pipe filled with charcoal and sand. Just thinking of that thin, brown liquid that we called drinking water gags me. Things do improve, Charley."

Ross sighed the last vestige of his anger away. "I wasn't sore at you, Mark. It's just the damned waiting."

"I know. Call me about sundown."

Ross's face was dubious. "Clell sounded like it was important."

"He can wait that long." Mark closed the door behind him.

He lived in a bare, little room with a cot and a flimsy chair. Nails driven into the wall took care of his clothes. He needed no more. He spent so little time in here anyway.

He lay down and squirmed into a more comfortable position. How could a man amass so many sore spots in just a few seconds? Ordinarily, the heat might have kept him awake. Today, it was only an additional soporific to his dull nerves.

When he awakened, he lay in a puddle of water on the cot. It hadn't been a refreshing nap. He felt jaded and dragged out.

He looked at his reflection in a broken piece of

mirror and shuddered. The colors were just beginning to show in their full glory. He thought sourly, I hope Larkson looks worse.

He swore as he discovered he was out of clean pants. He looked with distaste at the ones he'd slept in. He would have to wear them, for Charley didn't have any new ones in his size. At least he didn't have three weeks ago. His face brightened. Ross had had time to get in a new shipment by now.

He slipped into a fresh shirt and stepped out into the store. "You get my pants in, Charley?"

Ross shook his head. Something bigger than Mark's size was on his mind. "Mark, I want to say one more thing, then forget it. I didn't mean what I said about Clell."

Mark made an impatient gesture. It was a trying subject, and he wanted no more of it. "I know you didn't."

Ross plowed ahead. "Any man big enough to have the vision Clell had about this valley is beyond little people like me. While he goes about making that vision a reality, we try to pull him down."

Mark knew a little impatience. When Charley swung, he swung wide. He was clear on the other side now.

"To set the record straight, Charley, it wasn't Clell's vision first." He wondered why he said that. It wasn't important.

He shook his head at the surprise in Ross's face. "Wozencraft saw it first fifty years ago. He caught the significance of a vast plain lying below a river. He realized that all of those acres could be irrigated by gravity. But those sixteen hundred square miles were public land, and Wozencraft had to have the authority of Congress before he could act. Congress kept shoving the bill back, and Wozencraft's vision died under the treatment. Clell's just been more fortunate in his timing. That isn't taking any credit away from Clell. It took fifty years for another man to see it. And Clell's done something about it."

Clell Hodges had had his headaches over this thing. Mark knew, for he had been in with him from the start. Investors had weakened and dropped out from under him, and a couple of unscrupulous promoters had tried to cut up most of the melon for themselves. Maybe Clell had dented a couple of ethics, but he could be forgiven for that. A big dream drove a man hard.

Ross walked to the door with him. "And you're with him all the way."

"All the way."

"It'll cost you some lumps."

Mark knew that. Nobody was ever neutral about Clell. Hodges had a few close friends and many enemies. There was nothing in between. His passion to accomplish was an affront to the ordinary man. That leadership wasn't an affront

31

to Mark. He had accepted it in college, and it fitted him naturally. Clell had been a big man on campus, and Mark had been grateful for the bond that had formed between them. The bond hadn't weakened after graduation, and when Clell had written him, saying there was a job for him on the Yakima Valley irrigation project, Mark had jumped at the chance. That had been the first irrigation project in the Northwest, and Mark had learned as much about engineering under Hodges, as he had in his school courses. Hodges knew maps like another man knew the palm of his hand. He could translate those maps into plans for tearing land from the wilderness. Given a big problem Hodges could smash ahead with awing momentum. But when petty details hemmed him in, he bogged down and was lost. Hodges was such a complexity of nature. His hands were large enough to enfold a cantaloupe, yet they could set the fine adjustment on a transit with unfailing accuracy. He could withstand the roughest treatment a country could give him, yet personal criticism either angered or hurt him. His serious weakness was that he couldn't distinguish between friends and people who would use him. He couldn't learn to strike a balance, and each new disillusionment cut him to the core. Clell Hodges' brusqueness might irritate Mark, but it could never turn him.

He stood in the doorway, looking out at the

desert beyond the town. The desert put an insidious hold on a man. Its harshness never gentled much, but at evening there was a degree of softening. During the day, the savage glare blinded one to the desert's soft colors, but with a lessening of the sun's intensity the colors appeared; the purples of the mountains, the reds and browns of the valley floor, and a man was lost in discovering the beauty of them.

He loved his desert best from evening on. A breeze usually sprang up, giving the illusion of coolness, though the sand continued to give off its radiation of heat until well after midnight. The breeze stirred the grains of sand, and they slithered together, making a sound as though they talked in a dry, sibilant whisper. If a man listened closely enough, that whisper said something to him. Perhaps it took a special ear to catch its promise. Maybe Wozencraft had been the first with that special ear. Surely, Clell Hodges was the second.

He smiled at his fanciful roaming. "I'd better be getting on over to the hotel."

"You can wait and walk over with Clell." Ross pointed down the street, and Mark easily picked out Hodges' big figure among the foot traffic. Hodges always moved with long, vigorous strides. He was tall and big, and even in repose, an air of restlessness oozed out of him. He carried his blond head high, the stubborn chin thrust forward. He was a handsome man though he gave little awareness to his physical appearance. He was a doer in this world, and that class of men were always impatient of the existing limitations. A project this vast needed a Clell Hodges.

Ross sighed. "Sometimes he wears me out just watching him."

Mark smiled. It was an apt way to put it.

"Mark, tell him you just got in."

Mark gave him an astonished glance. "Why?"

"You know how he'll yell at the wasted time."

"I don't imagine a few hours will cost anybody too much."

Hodges saw them and increased his stride. He sprang up the two steps and seized Mark's hand. "It's good to see you, boy. When did you get in?"

Mark gave Ross a wicked glance to let him know how wrong he was. "Around noon. I grabbed a nap."

Hodges frowned at the discoloration in Mark's face. "Were you in an accident?"

"That's as good a way as any to put it. I ran into Larkson."

Hodges' jaw sagged. "You mean you were fighting with him?"

Mark touched his split mouth. "For a while I wasn't doing too much of it. I made a mistake with him."

A storm gathered in Hodges' face. "Fighting with a man like Larkson over some personal disagreement. Damn it, Mark. With everything we have to do—"

"It wasn't personal, Clell. Larkson mentioned he thought you were stealing the settlers' water money."

Hodges had the grace to color, but he didn't apologize. He never did. "If you had looked me up the moment you got into town, it wouldn't have happened. But you spent the rest of the afternoon sleeping."

Mark cut his eyes at Ross. Ross was returning that wicked glance with interest.

Mark slammed his temper back into place. "I was beat up. I earned this afternoon. I haven't taken an hour off in weeks."

"I'm not begrudging you the afternoon. It's only the bad timing of it. Chaffey leaves town for Los Angeles tonight. If we miss him—"

A fire burned in his eyes, and Mark had the uneasy feeling it was fed with malicious fuel.

Hodges threw an arm about his shoulders. "Now let's go beard the old bastard in his den."

Another disagreement between them, Mark thought dismally. And Hodges was drawing him into it. Between the two, he would be batted back and forth until he was reeling.

Mark waited until they had taken a few steps. "Clell, the gate's in."

"Good, good." Hodges' absent tone showed he had more important things on his mind.

"I disobeyed Chaffey's orders. I put the sill all the way to the floor of the canal. If you ever need additional water, all you have to do is to remove the flashboards I installed."

"Maybe Mr. Chaffey is through giving orders." There was an ugly ring in Hodges' voice.

A chilly wind of unease brushed Mark. Something big was on Hodges' mind, so big Mark doubted he had heard a word he said. He thought of repeating it and let it go. He would have to catch Hodges in a quieter moment.

Hodges strode into the hotel and asked the clerk at the desk, "Is Chaffey in?"

"Yes sir, Mr. Hodges."

"Good." Hodges turned and headed for the stairs. Mark was a half-dozen steps behind him by the time they reached the second floor.

Hodges pounded on the door, and Mark thought dryly, a little more force, and you could batter it down.

"Come in," a grumpy old voice called.

Hodges threw open the door and stepped into the room. He looked at the partially packed suitcase on the bed, and malice was noticeable in his face. "Going somewhere, Mr. Chaffey?"

"I told you I had to go to Los Angeles." The dislike was plain on Chaffey's face. His shoulders bowed under his better than sixty years, and his waist had thickened. His face was seamed and sagging, and his white hair was sparse. But the blue eyes were as keen and fierce as ever. He had a familiar, stubborn, belligerent jut to his chin, and Mark thought, I'm looking at Clell Hodges when he reaches Chaffey's age. It was small wonder that animosity flowed so strongly between them. They were too much alike.

Chaffey had some tremendous projects of his own behind him. He had started the great orange groves in Southern California, and he had been the irrigation genius who had built Mildura and Renmark in New South Wales. Hodges had found him in desperation when all his other backers had failed him, and Chaffey was the ideal man for this. He had capital, and he had experience. The thing that was lacking in this combination was harmony.

Chaffey swung his eyes to Mark. "Did you get the gate in?"

Mark nodded.

"It took you longer than I expected." Chaffey said it absently as though needing words to fill in an awkward void.

Mark wondered if he should tell about the lowered gate sills and held it. There was no place in this room for anything but the hostility that slammed back and forth between the two men.

Chaffey glowered at Hodges from under grizzled eyebrows. "Get on with it, man. I know you didn't come here to wish me Godspeed."

Hodges smiled. "Maybe I did."

Chaffey caught the threat, and his face tightened. "Say it plainer."

"You sold too much stock to your friends, believing they'd hold it. Now that everybody knows that this valley will be irrigated, they liked the higher price of their stock. They were willing to sell and take their profit. And luckily enough I found investors who wanted to loan money on a safe thing. Something that I lacked before. I've been busy, George."

Mark had never heard Hodges call Chaffey by his first name. There was no friendliness in his using it.

For a moment, Chaffey looked old and defeated, then his head lifted. "You have control, or you wouldn't be here."

"I have control. You can stay under my management, or I can raise enough money to buy you out."

"You mean I can stay and have you rub my nose in it. I've swallowed a lot of things, Hodges, but that is too bitter. Now I understand why it's taken you so long to get in the irrigation ditches. You've been too busy on other things. I looked this project over once and rejected it. But I was fool enough to come back."

Hodges tried to say something, and Chaffey cut him short. "It's my time to talk. This thing had a bad smell from the first. I didn't like the Alamo barranca bending southward and traveling forty

38

miles through Mexican soil before it came back to United States land. It gives two governments something to say about the water, and one is more than enough."

That unfortunate error in the boundary would crop up again and again. Mark had heard the legend of how it had happened, and he wouldn't be surprised, if it was true. American and Mexican officials had agreed upon a line running west from Texas to the Colorado River fifteen miles south of Yuma. It should have continued directly on from there, but a dispute arose in the surveying party, and the Mexicans refused to go on. The party adjourned to a saloon in Yuma, and the discussion grew friendlier as the drinks increased. The surveyors set up a transit near the bar and sighted the line through the screen door toward the mountains. It put a jog in the boundary, and the Alamo barranca, immediately after entering American territory, bent and meandered into Mexico.

"I'm getting old," Chaffey continued. "I had my eyes filled with a green valley, and I refused to see anything else. Hodges, you are a scoundrel. I thought so when I first heard about the options. You let me think you had them secured. It cost me twenty thousand dollars to Hall Hanlon alone. And General Andrade cost me some more. When the Alamo entered Mexico, it ran through his land, too."

Hodges' face burned a brick red. "I meant to tell you about those options. I'd forgotten they'd run out. Hanlon and Andrade saw a chance to hold you up, and they took it."

That was true, but Hodges in his desperation that Chaffey would back out of the project, had hidden the fact of the elapsed options. It wasn't the money as much as the duplicity that enraged the old man so. And he had struck back. One of his requirements was that he would have complete control of the Company, and he had treated Hodges contemptuously after that. Hodges' resentment had built until he choked on it. He honestly considered that Chaffey had taken his Company away from him.

"A damned scoundrel," Chaffey repeated. "No wonder I got so far off the road. I just ignored all the warning signs."

Hodges' face contorted. "You can't talk to me like that."

Mark watched them with troubled eyes. Chaffey's judgment was too harsh. Hodges had had no deliberate thought of cheating Chaffey. But after his struggle to raise capital, he had hung onto Chaffey by any desperate means he could use.

"I'll talk to you any way I choose. I could stay here and fight you. I could sure enough wreck the Company. But I don't think I have to. You'll do it yourself. Buy me out."

"Good!" Hodges whirled and plunged out of the room.

Chaffey checked Mark's leaving by thrusting out his hand. "We've had a good relationship. Are you going to continue working for him?"

Mark nodded. Chaffey had Hodges all wrong, and Mark wanted to make him understand. "Mr. Chaffey, if I could explain—"

Chaffey shook his head. "No use. It's over. Maybe I was too harsh on him. I can understand how a man can drive himself into a bind. Maybe that happened to him. But I want to give you some advice. He's a man of great vision, but he's wild and impractical in many ways. He'll plunge without taking a second look. Steer him as much as you can, or he'll wreck the Company and hurt a lot of people. Now if you'll let an old man finish his packing—"

Mark looked back from the door. Chaffey's hands were filled with his belongings, but his mind wasn't on his packing. It was far away, and a loneliness was in his face.

Mark shut the door. Hodges was pacing the lobby when he came downstairs, and he turned a furious face toward him. "Did he want you to stay so you could listen to his crying over his beating?"

Hodges wasn't as generous as Chaffey had been. "No. He admitted he'd been harsh on you."

"Hah." Surprise filled Hodges' face, then he

shook it off. "Now that I've got his dead weight off my back watch me tear up this desert." He whacked Mark on the back. "I'll show everybody."

You could have shown them before, Mark thought dully.

Hodges sensed the judging in him. "Don't you think I have a right? It was my dream. The Company's always belonged to me. You'll see it differently in the morning. Lord, I've got a million things to do. I'll see you in the morning." The wooden floor boomed under his bootheels.

It was hot in this lobby, yet Mark had the impulse to shiver as he watched him go. So now Hodges was going to run both the business and engineering end of this. And either side was big enough to absorb all a man's energies. It didn't have to be done this way, Clell, he thought miserably. It was big enough for both of you.

CHAPTER THREE

Hodges was out of sight by the time Mark reached the street. It suited him fine. He couldn't get the memory of a defeated loneliness in an old man's eyes out of his head. Hodges had made heavy demands on their friendship tonight.

"I need a drink," he muttered. "Or maybe two or three." He grinned wryly and stopped counting.

He would put no limitations on himself tonight.

When he stepped into the saloon, he thought he had picked the wrong one, for Larkson stood at the end of the bar. The room went silent, and Larkson turned his head and saw him. Maybe he didn't have as many bruises on his face as Mark, but Mark thought they were more massive. He met Larkson's eyes, and the rigidity that seized his muscles put a physical ache in them. But Larkson only nodded jerkily, and Mark returned it.

He sat down at a table, and talk picked up again. The hollow in his stomach rapidly filled. Maybe I should have welcomed further argument from him, he thought. Maybe I could've worked myself out of this mood. He looked at Larkson's broad back, and he knew the thoughts were just idle speculation. Bruises weren't something a man welcomely stacked up like poker chips.

He had his choice of warm beer or warm whisky, and the whisky seemed the least revolting. He sat sipping at his drink, but his eyes and thoughts were far away. He looked up, and William Holt was standing at his table.

Holt grinned. "When a man drinks alone, it's usually because he has no friends, or he's in a foul mood."

"A little of both with me, Bill."

"Then let's see if we can correct it." Holt pulled out a chair and sat down.

He was a tall, gangling man, and those thin arms and legs didn't quite seem to match his body. He came from Missouri, and the nasal twang of his origin was still in his voice. He had a lazy, nondescript face and indolent eyes, but they were only a cover for the energy that coursed through him. Mark had mistrusted him at first, for the man had a finger in every activity, and a man as sharp at making a dollar as Holt was usually earned a natural suspicion from his fellowman. That first estimation had been sadly wrong. Holt insisted upon making a profit on everything he went into, but he was no sharpshooter. He wanted the other man to make a profit, too. He loved to gamble on human beings, and he rarely made a mistake in judgment. Most of the businesses in town had Holt's financing behind them. Mark had never heard a belittling remark made about the man, and he thoroughly approved of him.

Holt tasted his whisky. "Why does a man drink this stuff in this weather? It only puts heat inside and outside of you at the same time. Want to talk about what's eating you?"

Mark wanted to, but he wouldn't. A man didn't discuss a fight with his wife with outsiders—and this was a family fight.

"Maybe it's for the best." Holt grinned at Mark's start. "I just put Chaffey on the stage to Flowing Well. He told me he's leaving the valley for good. He's a bitter old man."

"He told you all about it?" Mark was disappointed in Chaffey.

"Only what I told you he said. Hodges came to me a couple of weeks ago, asking me to put money in the Company. I agreed and took it out in water stock. I figured then what he was after. He's got control, hasn't he?"

Those indolent eyes missed nothing. Mark could see no practical advantage in denying it. By tomorrow, it would be all over town anyway. He nodded slowly.

"And you don't approve?"

"Do you?"

Holt sipped at his drink. "It's been coming for a long time. Anybody could see it. Those two aren't gaited to pull together. Each of them was too stiff-necked to give a little."

"It was big enough for both of them. Clell had to put the Company heavily in debt to swing it."

"He did. Don't you think he's man enough to cut it?"

Mark's lack of response was answer enough.

"I'd agree with you but for one thing. With or without Hodges, it won't fail now. It's too close to being an accomplished fact. If anything happens, somebody will step in and take it over."

Mark wondered if Holt had himself in mind, and he considered the possibility. It could even be a good thing. He put the disloyal thought out of his mind.

"Don't you think Clell can do it?"

Holt shrugged. "I'm no fortune teller. Maybe this breakup happened for the best. You'll see some progress now. Hodges will quit slowing down the work to embarrass Chaffey. And that will do all of us some good. Maybe Hodges is big enough to swing both ends. I hope so. But he's a fence jumper. One pasture never interests him for too long."

He stared hard at Mark. "Are you going to continue working for him?"

Mark scowled. Holt should know the answer to that. "Yes."

"Figured you would. It's too bad because I could've used you. There's one thing I'm afraid of that can happen. Hodges will be short of money. He'll have to turn away the very people we need most because they won't even be able to pay the government filing fee, let alone buy their water stock, because he can't give them credit. They'll come in here with nothing but a wagonload of children and household goods and a lot of willing hands. Given a little help, they'll make it. I was thinking of furnishing them filing fees and water stock as a loan with no down payment nor interest."

Mark's eyes were puzzled, and Holt grinned. "You don't see it? Trust a man, and ninety-nine percent will work like hell to prove that trust wasn't misplaced. They'll repay every cent of

46

that loan. You're wondering where I'll make any money out of that? I'll make it by building businesses to furnish the services those people will need. If we don't fill this valley with people, nobody will do a damned bit of good. I was hoping you'd help me get these people in here."

The offer had its appeal, but Mark didn't give it consideration. He knew his pasture and was content to stay in it.

Holt finished his drink and stood. "Keep it in the back of your head. A man never knows when things will change." He nodded his good night and ambled toward the door.

Mark watched him until he was out of sight. It was flattering to think that a man of Holt's standing would make this offer. But things would never change—not that much.

Suddenly, his gloom was gone. Holt was unperturbed at the shift in ownership. He saw beyond the petty squabbling of men. He anchored his eyes to a goal, and nothing switched him.

Mark didn't want another drink. He didn't even want the remainder of the whisky in the glass. In a way, Holt was an engineer, too. Only, he built with people. And maybe his was the biggest building of all. Mark felt lighthearted and vigorous again. Now when a penniless family approached him he wouldn't have to send them to Hodges for their turndown. He would steer them straight to William Holt. He thought again of Holt's offer. A man couldn't help but like a job like that. It must be a rewarding thing to see new hope dawning in a man's eyes.

CHAPTER FOUR

Twenty-four hours weren't enough in a day; not if a man wanted to use a few of them for sleep. For Hodges was driving men and animals like the devil ate on his tail. He covered fantastic distances, and nobody was certain where he would turn up next. Let a man take undue liberties with his job, and Hodges popped up behind him, his caustic tongue a sword severing men from jobs. He brooked no excuses, and he demanded just one thing: results. As angry as men grew at him still his flaming spirit inspired them to attempt to match his pace. And every man in the dozens of crews had the same desire —to see water flow through the ditches they were digging.

Hodges was as good as his word. He was literally tearing up the desert. Plows bit easily through the soft, unresistant sand, digging the cross laterals, and each day added more lines to its ancient face.

Colorado River water would come into the valley through two main canals, the New River and the Alamo barrancas. New River started at Cameron Lake on the Mexican border, meandered past Blue Lake, and wound into the arid Salton Basin. A canal connected the two barrancas for better control of the water, but the Alamo would carry the major portion.

Cross laterals ran every mile off of the main canal. Farmers would build their own distribution ditches, taking the water onto their land through wooden sluice gates the Company installed. Gravitational flow furnished enough head to insure a good flow to every corner of the field to be irrigated.

Irrigation would consist of putting several inches of water on a field and letting it soak in. When a farmer was ready for water, the Company would send around a Mexican *zanjero* to measure it. The measurer would raise the sluice gate so many inches for just so long and compute the units of acre-feet by a simple formula. An acre of ground, covered one foot deep, made an acre-foot, and it cost the farmer fifty cents. Average crops would need about four acre-feet a year, and a farmer would consider it cheap for the bounty he would receive in return. For every ingredient was here to insure only bumper harvests, the richness that Nature had slowly built up over the hundreds of centuries without any demands being drawn against it, the sun that blazed fiercely day after day without a break for months, and the sacks of seed ready to be opened. Rich land, sun, and seed. All that needed was the water. Men prophesied that within a week after the water was turned into the valley it would be green. Mark didn't think they were far wrong.

He stretched and yawned. Lord, he was tired, tired past the point of being able to sleep. All around him his crew was stretched out on the sand. The cooking fire was dying, letting the men blend back into the night shadows. Here and there, the winking eyes of cigarettes broke the black cast, and conversation was desultory. Mark had a good crew, all Mexicans but with a capacity for work. From beside the wagon he heard Lupita, Tomás Ceron's wife, singing. She sang one of the sad, haunting Mexican love songs, and it might have been imagination, but he thought she put too much yearning into it. It had been a shock when Tomás brought her to camp a month ago. Ceron was at least sixty years old, and Mark doubted that Lupita was twenty. She had a certain prettiness, but her eyes were too bold, too restless. He was quite aware of how they had weighed him.

Tomás had explained it as best as he could. "When I went back to visit my family, I found that Gonzales, my old friend, was dying. And dying badly because of his worry about his daughter. I promised him I would give her what help I could." His eyes had glowed with a delighted wonder. "It is not possible, Señor Addison, but she found love for an old man. She cried so hard I could not leave her."

Mark doubted that it had happened exactly that way. Tomás had a job, and Lupita had been frightened at her lack of prospects. That was the practical answer to that age discrepancy.

Tomás had said she was a good cook, and Mark had hired her. She was a bad cook, but he kept her on because of Tomás. He was glad this phase of the work was over, he was glad his contact with her would be broken. She was in the prime of her youth with a lush figure that she was careless about displaying. She wore peasant blouses with nothing beneath them, and they were constantly slipping from her shoulder. How many times had he caught her in a bending or stooping pose that showed all the riches beneath that blouse? And how many times had she laughed at his reddening face while her eyes mocked him?

Tomás would pay for his brief happiness, for he couldn't hold her. He might have had a better chance, if she had been thirty, for she would be fat by then. Already, the ample but plain fare had padded her figure with a few pounds. Mark was sorry about Tomás' coming heartache, but there was nothing anybody could do for him.

Tomás flipped away his finished cigarette. Mark watched its glowing arc and the explosion of its sparks against the sand.

"They let the water in this morning." Tomás made it half question, half statement.

"Yes." Mark didn't sound happy about it. He had hoped to be there to see it. For weeks he had been driving with that goal in mind, but he hadn't made it. He had another day's work ahead, and by the time it was done the water would be running strongly in the canals. Mark had badly wanted to see the first water flow through the Chaffey gate and be absorbed by the thirsty sand. That would be the biggest milestone the valley would ever know. The water would push down the canal in rolling bounds, and voices all along the Alamo would announce its coming. Tonight would be a gala time in Imperial. Mark guessed he was grumpy because he was going to miss the celebration.

Tomás shifted his position on the sand. "I hope it will be a good thing." He wore rough denim clothing and a ragged straw hat. His footwear was rawhide soles, held in place by thongs that ran between the toes and tied about the ankles. His face was hewn to weathered skin over an angular skull, and constant exposure to the sun and a natural inclination toward swarthiness had turned him almost black. He had the liquid, velvet eyes of the Mexican race, and his manner was self-effacing but not cringing. He was a simple man with a pureness of simplicity that had its own dignity.

His words surprised Mark. "How can it be anything else but good?"

Tomás took a long time with his answer. "I do not know. I hear you talk about how someday all this will be green, but if God intended it that way, would not He have so made it?"

Mark wondered how many hours Tomás had pondered over this? "He intended it this way, Tomás. He built enough green spots for men to start with. But as more men came, He left spots like this for them to develop."

Tomás still wasn't convinced. "All my life I have lived around that river. It is a mad bull. I do not believe any man can chain it."

Tomás' words put no apprehension in Mark. The Colorado might roar and bellow, but they had chained it.

"It's chained, Tomás."

Lupita's laugh rang out, and Tomás turned his head toward it. "Am I not lucky to have such a one?"

He was constantly aware of her. Mark had noticed it before. "She's lucky to have you."

"No, señor. A man my age does not find someone like her." He shook his head and picked up the thing that troubled him. "You know where the ancient sea is?"

Mark nodded. Tomás referred to the great, arid depression called the Salton Basin. The Southern Pacific tracks crossed through the sink just before they reached Flowing Well. The Salton Basin was a vast, shallow depression stretching farther than the eye could reach. The sun blazed on the great patches of white, where the salt from an ancient sea had collected, and blinded the eye.

"Once, the sea was there, señor."

Tomás didn't know it, but the sea had been there several times, perhaps at intervals of five hundred years apart. Each time the river capriciously changed its course, the sink filled. When the river went back to its old bed, the sun evaporated the water. Men figured it had been dry now since 1540. Diaz had recorded the perils of crossing the burning waste, and some two hundred years later, de Anza had written the same thing.

"There is a story about the time when the sea was there, señor. Would you like to hear it?"

Mark would. He was always interested in folk legends. Though most of them had been fancifully embroidered through the years, some basis was in them.

"The sea was bountiful then, señor. Fish swam in it, and plants grew about its edges. The Mojaves lived on one shore, the Cocopahs across the sea from them. Each year, the Cocopahs plundered the Mojaves. They took their food and carried away the most beautiful of their women. It went on until the Mojaves rebelled. They ambushed the Cocopahs, and the slaughter was a terrible thing. Not a single Cocopah survived. The Mojaves took everything the Cocopahs had. And it showed them the way to an easier life. Why plant and hunt and fish? Other tribes would do that for them. The Mojaves would live by plundering."

Mark lit his pipe. Tomás believed his story. It showed in his expression.

"Many ships, filled with a once peaceful people, set out across the sea. But the Great White Spirit saw the evil intentions in their hearts. He sent a terrible wind. It turned the day black, and its whistling tongue lashed the sea to fury. The waves rose higher and higher until not a ship remained, not a Mojave was left alive. The next morning, the sea was gone, and only the great dry hole remained."

Mark was puzzled as to why Tomás had told him this legend, but he waited.

"It is said the sea will come again, if men have evil intentions. It will come and destroy everything man has built. And you have opened the door to it."

Mark understood now. "It won't come again, Tomás. Where are the evil intentions?"

Tomás sighed. "There are always evil intentions in men's hearts." He might have said more, but Lupita called, "Tomás." Her voice was always shrill when she called him.

Tomás smiled abashedly and got to his feet.

"Her tongue wags faster when I do not go to her."

Mark watched him walk away. The legend kept running through his mind. Both he and Tomás feared the river but not from the same basis. Tomás' fear was based on superstition, his on fact and knowledge, but how far apart were they? He knocked out his pipe and smiled ruefully. He must make sure there were no evil intentions in his heart.

Mark finished a couple of hours earlier than he figured, and the crew reached Imperial before dark the following day. Last night must have been a big one, for he could still see the marks of the celebration in men's faces. He had never seen so much activity. Men no longer stood on the corners and talked aimlessly. Now they had something to do, and already they were too far behind.

He caught the new momentum that had seized the town. Everything was rushed now. Men rushed into stores and back out. They were lined up before the bank, but even in that, Mark sensed a surging sense of rush. They were impatient to get this business over and get on with something else.

They passed him in a rush, and they didn't pause long enough to exchange a few words. He got a nod or a wave, or at best a flung, "Hello."

He passed Adams coming out of Ross's store, and Adams's back was bent under the heavy burden of a seed sack. Mark gave him a hand swinging it up into the wagon.

Adams grinned sheepishly. "She's running in the canal north of town, Mark. That damned Larkson didn't know what he was talking about."

It was the only apology Mark would ever get, and it was enough. "Are you ready to plant, Adams?"

Adams's swearing was directed at himself. "I haven't even cleared all my land. I stood around and screamed with the rest when I could have been working. I rushed here now to buy my seed because I think Charley's going to be out damned soon. And he won't be able to freight in enough to keep up with the demand. If I only had that damned greasewood cleared." He moved to the wagon seat and swung up on it. "I gotta be at it." He waved a friendly hand and drove off.

Mark smiled as he watched the wagon recede. It was better this way. His face sobered. Adams had a problem, as did all the others. Those tough, little greasewood bushes had long catclaw roots that clung to the desert soil. It took a team of horses and a chain to pull them out one at a time. After that slow, tedious work, the land had to be leveled so that the irrigation water could cover all of it. Removing the greasewood left holes that had to be filled and hummocks that had to be smoothed. Adams wouldn't be alone in wishing he had his land prepared.

Mark turned toward the canal north of town. He hadn't seen the water come into the valley, but he could watch it flowing in its canal. And that would be second best.

As he moved away from the store, he thought he heard Ross call after him. He didn't pause nor turn his head. Whatever Ross wanted could wait until after he had seen the water.

Women lined the bank of the canal dipping water out of it. The sun clubbed at them with its fierce afternoon rays, but not a face showed the usual discomfort. They had water, unlimited water within a stone's throw of town, and this was luxury, this was easy living.

The water carried a good portion of sand, but at least half of that would settle, if left standing for a few hours. The remaining pearl gray liquid would scour a pan bright with a few swipes. Mrs. Clawson offered a cup to Mark, and he accepted it without hesitation. The water had a faint, gritty taste.

He ran his tongue against his teeth and grinned. "It ought to keep your teeth white. Until it wears through the enamel."

He couldn't say anything against this water that would dismay her. "I don't care. It's water, and I don't have to guard every drop."

Mark thought of the fifty-mile trip it had made

through Mexico, and of all the things people along the way might have dumped into it. But it ran through sand, and wasn't sand supposed to purify water every so many feet? No matter what pictures he could conjure up against it, it couldn't be as bad as that Blue Lake water.

"If I can borrow your cup again." He bent to dip up another cupful.

He stayed there until almost dark, fascinated by the sight and sound of the running water. Much of what ran in the canal would be wasted, eventually draining off into the Salton Basin, for the farmers weren't ready for it. But that didn't matter. Wasn't there an unlimited supply where this came from?

All around him he saw clouds of dust rising into the sky. Plows made that dust as farmers attacked the hummocks and hollows, leveling the land. Even the stubborn, little greasewood bushes added their puff of dust, as their roots were torn free. Mark frowned as he thought about it for a moment. There should be an easier and faster way to clear the land.

Those farmers would work from light to dark and begrudge the night's coming. A man wouldn't count his weariness though it dragged at his every step. There would be time enough to rest after the seed was in.

He walked back toward town. He could see no physical difference in it, but it had changed magically in a few hours. It hummed and vibrated with new purpose and energy, and he thought, it wasn't buildings that made a town; it was attitude. The people would come now, they would come in great droves. He remembered his conversation with Bill Holt. Holt had called it as though he had seen an actual blueprint of it. He had that rare gift of foresight, and he would prosper immensely by it. Mark thought of Holt's offer with a small wistfulness. Any associate of Holt's would prosper in direct ratio. He shook his head, and the wistfulness faded. He was no fence jumper.

Ross's door was locked, but a light was on inside. Mark hammered on the door. "Open up, Charley."

"Go away. I'm closed."

"Goddamit. It's me, Mark."

It seemed a long time before he heard the sound of Ross's footsteps. It wasn't like Ross to close while there might still be some business around. Either of two reasons could be the cause; Ross was sick, or drunk. Mark discarded the second. Ross wasn't that hard a drinking man. He worried about the first all the time it took Ross to cross the floor and open the door.

Ross looked like hell. He had a sort of caved-in look about his face as though he had suffered a numbing blow. His eyes were vacant, and his mouth was too slack. He also had a bottle in his left hand, and Mark booted all his worries away. He had never seen it before, but Charley Ross was well on his way to getting drunk.

Ross looked accusingly at him. "I yelled at you a couple of hours ago."

"I heard you. I was afraid Hodges wanted me."

"Not Hodges. Me. I needed you."

Mark imagined Ross had wanted a drinking companion. Now he figured Mark had turned him down, and with a drunk's fretfulness, he picked at it, enlarging it out of all proportions.

Mark grinned at the bottle in Ross's hand. "It looks like you're doing all right without me."

Ross's eyes were outraged. "Damnit. I'm not drunk."

Mark gave him a closer inspection. Ross was right. But something was riding him.

A man started to enter behind Mark, and Ross shoved him back. "I'm closed." He slammed and locked the door.

"I had to close. I couldn't keep my mind on anything."

There was an unconscious plea for sympathy in Ross's voice.

He hoisted himself up on a counter. "All right, Charley. What's it all about?"

Ross handed him a letter. It was limp and rumpled as though it had been read several times. "This came shortly before I yelled at you. Go on. I want you to read it."

Mark read the short letter rapidly. "Mother died in her sleep. I would like to see you. If you don't want me to come, telegraph me. Otherwise, I will arrive at Flowing Well on the twenty-sixth." It was signed, Amity.

Mark looked at the calendar. "That's tomorrow."

"Don't I know it? Look at the date on that letter. It was written over two weeks ago. The post office must've misplaced it." He cursed the mail until he was out of breath.

Mark waited for him to run down. "Who is Amity?"

"My daughter. I haven't seen her for ten years. If that damned letter had only been delivered in time."

Mark realized something with a mild shock. "You would have wired and told her not to come."

Ross made a helpless gesture. "What else could I do? We're strangers. What can I say to her?"

"Tell me about it." The loneliness Mark had seen so often in Ross's eyes had a basis.

"There's little to tell. I came to the desert ten years ago for my health. Her mother refused to come with me. I sent her money in every letter I wrote, and I never stopped begging her to come out here. She never answered."

Mark tapped the letter. "What are you going to do about this? You can't leave her sitting at Flowing Well."

"Meet her for me, Mark." The pleading was back in Ross's voice. "I can't get away. I can't close the store."

"You closed it tonight."

"Oh, my God. Mark, you've got to do it. I'm afraid to meet her. I know I have to see her sooner or later. But I'd like to clean up the store. It'd give me a little more time to think."

Mark nodded. Ross wanted to see her. It was written all over his face. And a fear was there, too, a fear at his daughter's possible judging.

"I'll tell Theobold to have a team and buggy ready shortly after sunrise, Charley." It was forty miles to Flowing Well, and he could have most of the trip behind him in the relatively cooler hours of the day. He wouldn't let himself think about the return trip. He could make it. He didn't know about the girl.

"Mark, I'll never forget this. I'm in your debt forever."

"Oh, shut up. You get this store and yourself cleaned up. And put that damned bottle away. And welcome her, Charley. Welcome her like you should."

Ross looked as if he was about to cry.

Mark turned abruptly for the door. "I'll see you before I go. I've got to see Theobold and Hodges. I want to tell Clell I'll be gone all day tomorrow."

He had to fight his way through the press of people to get into Hodges' office. Each time he tried to interrupt, Hodges brushed him aside to take another man's congratulations. His laughter boomed out again and again, and his eyes shone.

Mark watched with a curious detachment. Clell's big moment no doubt was running over from last night. Mark didn't begrudge him the length: Hodges had earned it.

Hodges finally turned to him, and Mark had never seen him in a more expansive mood. "Nothing can stop me now, Mark. By God, I did it."

He made it sound like a single man's accomplishment. Mark thought of the hundreds of men who had had a hand in this. He had done a little of that work himself.

"Did you want to see me about anything important, Mark?"

"I just came in to congratulate you." Hodges wouldn't even miss him tomorrow.

"Fine, fine." He turned back to his waiting well-wishers.

Mark stared at the broad back for a moment from the doorway. Hodges was big in triumph. Mark wished he could have been a little charitable along with it.

CHAPTER FIVE

Theobold had picked Mark a spanking good pair of bays, and while the buggy wasn't new it was tight. He made as good time as the road would allow, for by any standards it was a rough one. He should know. Building it had been his first job, and expedience had been the measurement, not pride. Fresnos and plows had scraped a raw scar across the face of the desert. The scar ran through dry washes and gullies, some of them thirty feet deep, and skirted the ones it couldn't cross. It handled a considerable amount of traffic, for all supplies for the valley had to come over it. Now with the coming of water the traffic would jump. He tried to imagine what this valley would look like a year from now.

To most people, the desert was a monotonous horror with nothing to change this minute from the one gone by. Some men never became attuned to the desert's moods, and it was hell on most women. It was never gentle, but a man could learn to live with it. Its vegetation was scanty, and each stunted bit of growth showed its struggle to live. Only the hardier plants such as the creosote bush and mesquite trees could make it at all. But around the rare oases screw bean, palo verde, and California palm grew in abundance, and the salt weed abounded along the damp stretches of the barrancas. They were good for little, but they were living proof that things could grow here.

He let the team settle into a smooth pace that ate up the miles but still didn't put too much drain on them. He sat there, cursing his agreement to meet Ross's daughter. He hadn't even thought to ask her age. Ross had said he left ten years ago. The letter was proof against the thought that Amity might still be a child. It was simple but direct, the product of a mature mind. He remembered the unconscious appeal in it, but she hadn't begged or demanded. He found himself nodding in approval at that.

He felt a sudden surge of violence. "Damn it." He had no business in this. Ross was asking too much.

The sun gathered more force, and Mark let the team's pace slacken. He had started in good time, and there was no need to rush.

It was hot by the time Flowing Well swam into view through the heat haze. The name was a misnomer. It was the briefest of stops for the Southern Pacific en route to Yuma. But it was important to Imperial Valley. It consisted of a frame hotel of four rooms with its partitioning walls made of muslin sheets slid along wires. It had a tent on a platform, a corral, and three adobe huts with their ever-present complement of naked Mexican kids playing about them. The water tank was the most important item, a huge, wooden tank on stilts which the railroad kept replenished from tank cars. The railroad had tried to drill a well here, and the driller's report had said, "She's dry all the way to China." During the blazing hours of the afternoon, that tank water was almost hot enough to shave with. Even in the relative cool of the early morning, it was tepid and flat to the taste. Mark would take the ditch water flowing out of the Colorado any time.

He pulled out his watch and glanced at it. He sighed at what it told him. He was two hours early, even if the train was on time. And only a believer in fairy tales would expect that.

He pulled up beside McCaulley's hostelry, and McCaulley came out to greet him. McCaulley was a stringy man with the stamp of the desert on him. Mark never did know his age. The aging process seemed to stop at a certain point in the desert, and a man just grew more leathery. It was a healthy climate, for the old-timers seemed to have as much drive as a young man.

"Hello, Mark." McCaulley looked at the team and nodded approval. They weren't lathered bad at all. "I'll water and give them a feed."

He unbuckled the harness and led them away. Mark followed and watched him supervise the animals' drinking. He didn't allow them all the water they wanted. After they ate, they could drink again.

The east side of the corral made sparse bands of

shade, and McCaulley led them to it. He poured oats into the feed trough. "Heard the water reached Imperial."

Mark nodded.

"I'll bet that was something to see."

"It was." Mark squinted up the tracks. They blazed like a double line of fire until they disappeared in the glare of alkali to the north. A man's eyes swam if he looked at those blinding white patches too long.

That alkali worried him. There was a lot of it around, particularly around Imperial. What effect would it have on the crops?

"With water, business will be booming. You meeting somebody, Mark?"

"Charley Ross's daughter."

McCaulley looked surprised. "Hell, I didn't even know he was married."

Mark didn't go into it. That was Ross's affair. "Think the train will be on time?"

"I can remember once when she was. Let's see. That was ten or twelve years ago."

Mark grinned. "You're a funny man."

McCaulley cackled. "She's been doing pretty good lately, Mark. This is going to be an important stop before long."

So McCaulley saw it too. The trickle of humanity that had been coming through here would swell to a tide. The railroad might even consider building a proper hotel here.

"I get a kick out of their faces, Mark, when they step off the train. They see what's here, and they look sick."

It would be a terrible shock to anybody. "You've got a grisly sense of humor."

McCaulley's grin broadened. "I ran out of cold beer just before you came. I can give you a cup of coffee."

Mark nodded. That would be better than the water from the tank. Flowing Well was going to be a shock to Ross's daughter, also. Mark hadn't looked at the postmark of her letter, but wherever she was from, it couldn't be as bad as this. She might take one look, then get right back on the train. He speculated about that, wondering if it would be better or worse for Ross. Either way, Ross already had his jolt. And either way, he could never go completely back to his old way of living.

The coffee was as Mark remembered McCaulley's coffee, strong and tasting slightly of mud. It didn't make him any hotter, but it did make him drowsy, either that or last night's short hours of sleep were catching up with him.

He set down his empty cup. "Let's go outside."

"It won't be any cooler," McCaulley warned.

Maybe not, but the illusion would be there. The air under this canvas roof was stifling.

He stretched out in the shade on the east side of the frame building. McCaulley sat cross-legged beside him. He was hungry for news, and Mark's answers grew more and more drowsy.

"Hell, you don't tell a man nothing." McCaulley heaved to his feet.

Mark's eyes were closed before he was around the corner of the building.

The metallic rattle running through the rails awakened him. The sound carried a long way for the train wasn't yet in sight. But it would be soon.

It came in blasting and snorting, and for a moment Mark thought it was going on by. Then he saw the wheels spit out sparks as the brake shoes bit deep.

The passengers bolted out of the two coaches as soon as the train stopped. Mark couldn't blame them for that. That ride from Los Angeles must have been a taste of hell.

He watched each female face anxiously. Amity Ross would be traveling alone, and the two women's faces he saw didn't fit at all. Both of them were well into their middle age, and by their unhappy expressions he wouldn't want to spend a trip to Imperial with them. The second of the two paused at the steps and looked back into the coach.

"Jed, are you going to get off or not?"

A little, browbeaten-looking man followed her down the steps, and Mark thought that if he'd been that man, he would've stayed on the train.

Then the conductor appeared in the doorway.

He turned his head to somebody behind him. "Watch your step, miss."

He stepped down to the platform and held up a hand to aid her. He had a silly smile plastered all over his face.

Mark sucked in his breath as the woman paused before she descended. She was tall for a woman, but she carried it proudly. She looked as wilted as the rest of the passengers but with a vast difference. It didn't affect her serenity.

She placed her hand lightly on the conductor's arm and came down the steps. She thanked him with a smile, and he considered himself a lucky man.

She looked around, and there was no helplessness in her attitude. Instead, she was curious and interested.

He felt a queer excitement rising in him. He had seen truly beautiful women before, and this one wasn't in that class. Her mouth was too generous, her cheekbones too high and prominent. But then he saw that he was wrong in assessing each feature for its own perfection. That was like looking at a fine oil painting too close up and saying, the brush marks are too heavy, too coarse. The excitement was increasing, and he thought with a strange wonder, I wouldn't want her looking any different.

She had a wealth of dark auburn hair, in certain light it would look almost black, but now the sun brought out all its radiant glory. He had noticed how easily she moved as she came down the steps. There was a grace in this woman, and he suspected it would show in everything she did.

She kept turning her head as though expecting to see a familiar face, and no panic touched her composure when she didn't.

Her eyes rested briefly on Mark then drifted on.

He whistled soundlessly. Her eyes were magnificent. He couldn't say exactly what their color was. Certainly, there was green in them, and a shade of hazel, and perhaps a degree of blue, and he'd bet they would change colors with her moods. This couldn't be Amity Ross. It wasn't possible that Charley could produce something like this.

He approached her and touched the brim of his hat. "Miss Ross? Miss Amity Ross?"

He was a complete stranger to her, and he had known women who would have seized this moment as a pretext for being affronted. He half expected to see some sign of it in her.

She gave him an impersonal smile. "Why, yes."

Her eyes were almost on a level with his. He couldn't be more than a couple of inches taller than she. She had fine teeth, startlingly white and strong looking for a woman.

He laughed in sudden delight, not quite knowing the reason. "Charley sent me to meet you. I'm Mark Addison."

She extended a hand, and relief showed in her eyes. "I'm glad you came, Mr. Addison."

He could say, so am I, and mean it.

"Charley's a busy man. He's sorry he couldn't come. He's anxious to see you."

She let out a soft sigh, and he realized there had been fear in her. "When I didn't hear from him, I was almost afraid to come ahead."

"Your letter was just delivered to him yesterday."

"Oh." Her dismay was quick. "Then he might not—"

"Want you?" He shook his head at the absurdity of the thought.

"It's been such a long time." She wasn't quite assured.

That first meeting would be tough on both of them. They would be practically strangers to each other.

He wouldn't let her dwell on it. "Welcome to Imperial Valley, Miss Ross. We can offer you heat and sunshine and dust. But I can promise you we'll do better."

Her laughter rang out gay and free. "I come from south Texas, Mr. Addison. This isn't unknown to me."

But not to this degree, he thought. He didn't put it into words. She would find out for herself soon enough.

"Imperial's a booming city, Miss Ross. After

this, it will be a pleasant surprise. Why we even have running water. Of course, it's in a canal outside the town."

She showed her familiarity with arid countries. "Then it will grow."

"We can eat supper here and stay the night and drive in the cool of the morning. Or we can go on tonight, if you're not too tired."

"Oh, let's go on."

Supper was chili beans and coffee, both hot enough to take the skin off a tongue. She ate with good appetite, and he liked that. She adapted to conditions with no fuss.

McCaulley announced to the rest of the travelers, "Stage for Imperial will be here in the morning." He owned the stage line, and he missed no opportunities in scheduling. His hotel would be full tonight.

Mark smiled. "A man has to take every chance he can to pick up a dollar."

She nodded, her eyes dancing. "I have seen it before."

She would fit into this country, he decided. Her company put a new zest into the awful meal, and he cleaned his bowl.

Only the rim of the sun showed over the mountain as he finished harnessing. She watched its sinking with rapt attention. "The mountains are changing colors."

"The best time of the day," he agreed.

He stowed her luggage and helped her into the buggy. "May I drive?" she asked.

He should have been reluctant to turn over the reins, but somehow he had no qualms. The moment she started out he saw she knew what she was doing. She handled a team well with strong, competent hands. She kept them down to an easy pace and made no wearing demands on them. If she had known the road and her strength was equal to it, he would have been content to have her drive the entire way.

"It's a rough road, Miss Ross. Even though I built it."

"All of it?"

He nodded and thought wryly, you got that in, didn't you? He was a small boy making a brag to impress somebody. "I'm an engineer. Before we're through all of this waste will be useful."

She was a good listener, and he couldn't believe that all of these words were pouring out of him. His tone changed as he told her about the river. "It's the most destructive river in America. But we've chained it. It's fast water, and it carries the sand and soil it's cut from half a continent. It can slice through sand so fast it scares you."

"You sound as though you fear it."

He thought about it for a moment. "I do. Throw so much as a single pebble into the Colorado, and you might change the face of geography. That tiny pebble makes a riffle on the smooth bottom, the riffle soon builds into a sand bar, the bar starts an eddy, and the eddy turns into a whirlpool. Then the whole river pitches in, goes wild, and strikes in all directions. How can a man watch every pebble?"

"You give it personal characteristics."

"One of my men calls it a mad bull that only submits to its chains because it knows that it can throw them off any time it pleases. Sometimes I think he's right. I've listened to that river, and I swear it's chuckling at man's puny efforts."

"I'd like to see your river."

"And I'd like to show it to you."

She wouldn't let him remain silent. A skillful question would start him again. He told her all about Clell Hodges, and he didn't realize he was building him up so until she said, "You make him sound like a giant."

"He is. An ordinary man would've quit long before now. He's beaten heartache, frustrations, and unbelievable obstacles."

"I'd like to meet your Mr. Hodges, too."

"You will." He couldn't keep all of the flatness from his voice. He could have told her of the petty side of Clell Hodges, of his resentment to criticism, of his unwillingness to share credit. He wisely held his words, knowing how childish and petty they would sound.

"Tired?" he asked.

"A little."

He took the reins from her. He was amazed at the distance they had covered. Time flew when a man had a pretty and interested listener.

He glanced at her. "We haven't talked about you." He was aware of her small shrug.

"There isn't much. It's been ten years since I've seen my father. I was ten years old when he left, and I remember crying myself to sleep night after night."

He had an answer to an important question. She was twenty years old. He didn't pry. This was in the realm of personal business, and at the least it had left scars.

"Mother was impatient with me." Her voice was far away, and she stared straight ahead. "Mother was wrong. She was wrong about so many things."

He wished Charley could have heard that, and he ventured the wish. "I think he'd like to hear that."

She gave him a searching glance. "He will."

She fell silent, and he respected it. The miles slid behind them, and he noticed her head nodding. But each time she came to with a start.

"I'm so sleepy," she apologized.

He wanted to suggest she put her head on his shoulder, and he didn't dare. He slowed the pace of the team even more, wanting no jolt to slam into her. It would take longer to reach Imperial, but he didn't mind.

Her head sagged toward him and finally rested on his shoulder. He sat very still afraid that even his breathing would disturb her. He was filled with a crazy, cockeyed delight for which there was no explanation. He only hoped he would know it forever.

His shoulder was stiff and aching when the dark buildings of Imperial came into view. He pulled up before Ross's store, and the cessation of movement awakened her.

"Imperial. We're here."

She made no simpering apologies for her position. "I'm grateful for your shoulder. I can recommend it."

"I'd appreciate that." His smile was steady, but his throat felt tight. It didn't happen this way, not at first sight. But it wasn't first sight, he argued. He'd spent quite a stretch of hours in her company.

He indicated the light in Ross's store. "It looks as though Charley waited up for us." A dismaying thought struck him. What if Ross hadn't put that bottle away. I'll kill him, he thought savagely.

He opened the door, and Ross was at the far end of the room. He seemed unable to move, and his face was frozen in some kind of agony.

Father and daughter stared at each other a long moment, and an understanding passed between them, an understanding greater than any words could have built.

Ross had put away the bottle. He wore his best, and he had tried to slick down what little hair he had. Mark had never seen the store look this clean.

"Amity." The word was hoarse and cracked. Ross followed it with a stumbling step.

"Father." She rushed toward him.

Mark would be damned if Ross wasn't going to cry again. He backed slowly out of the door. It would be best if he spent the little remaining of the night at the hotel. He should have been tired, but his step was light and springy as he went toward the buggy.

CHAPTER SIX

It was after nine in the morning before Mark went back to the store. He had awakened early, but he thought he should give Amity and Charley a decent interval together before he butted in on them. He had the most logical reason in the world to go back to the store. Everything he owned was in that back room.

He heard Ross's voice before he stepped through the door. "But I told you I cleaned everything yesterday."

He saw Mark and shook his head. "Look at her. Hardest-headed daughter a man ever had."

Amity was on her hands and knees working

with a scrub brush in a corner. She had a bandanna knotted about her hair, and she wore one of Charley's aprons. She made no apology for her appearance, and Mark doubted she was even aware of it.

She smiled at him. "He claims he cleaned yesterday. Look at this." She made a swipe with the brush, and it left a muddy wake. "I'm talking about clean clean."

"She even counts the corners on me." His face was mournful, but his eyes were shining. They hadn't had much time together, but evidently, they hadn't needed much to find what flowed between them.

Amity stood and pulled the bandanna from her head. She shook her head, and her hair had a special magic in it for it fell into place. She untied the apron and laid it on the counter. "Don't think the cleaning's over. We've only started."

Ross groaned in mock misery.

"I came to take you two to breakfast," Mark said.

"Oh, we've eaten." Her face was filled with small regret. "Hours ago."

Ross patted his stomach. "I'd forgotten what good cooking tasted like. I've been doing my own too long."

Mark felt a big regret. He should have obeyed his impulse and gone to the store earlier.

Before he could say it, Hodges came into the

store. His face was angry, and for a moment he saw only Mark.

"Where in the hell were you yesterday? I looked for you all day."

Ross threw a veiled glance at Mark. "Blame me, Clell. I asked him to meet my daughter at Flowing Well. Amity, this is Clell Hodges."

Hodges looked as though he was in mild shock. He stared at her until a faint blush touched her cheeks, and now Mark was suddenly angry.

"I didn't even know you were married, Charley." Not once had Hodges taken his eyes from her. "Hello, Amity."

"Hello—" She hesitated just a fraction, "Clell. I heard a great deal about you."

Hodges moved to her, a smile on his face. "I hope all of it wasn't bad."

"It wasn't."

Mark felt a growing numbness. They had reached a first name basis immediately. He hadn't called her Amity during all the hours he had known her. She watched Hodges' face with an absorbed attention, and a petty protest filled Mark's mind—he stands over her more than I do. Something was happening, some vitally strong flow was passing between them. He felt suddenly shut out as though a thick glass wall had been erected between him and them. No, he yelled in violent protest, a protest that only he heard.

Hodges took her arm. "Have you seen our town yet?"

She shook her head.

"Then let me show it to you. I'm proud of the town I built."

The bitter protest swelled in Mark. Hodges used the personal pronoun too often.

Amity glanced at her father, and Ross nodded, but his face was blank.

Her happy laughter rang out, and the color remained in her face. "But I should fix up a little."

Hodges shook his head. "That would be gilding the lily."

He started for the door, then paused as though a thought just struck him. "Mark, I want you to ride out to the gate and see if the water's coming in fast enough to carry the sand away. If it isn't, we're going to have a silting problem." His eyes were sharp and intense. "I'd like to have a report as soon as possible."

Couching it in soft words didn't hide the blunt order. Mark was afraid to say anything. If he gave them the slightest opening, that torrent of hot words in his throat would pour out. He could only nod numbly.

He stared at the floor after they'd left. Her laughter drifted back to him. Hodges was using his charm. He had a sudden, violent impulse to destroy something.

He glanced at Ross, and Ross's face was savage. "Do you know what's the matter with you?" Ross shouted. "You're too civilized for your own good. You just stood there with your tongue in your mouth and let him do as he damned pleased."

He had only let Hodges do what he couldn't prevent. Her mute consent to Hodges had fashioned Mark's course for him. "Shut up, Charley. Just shut up."

Ross was in an argumentative mood. He opened his mouth, looked at Mark's eyes, then decided against saying what was in his mind. All the way to his room, Mark heard him muttering.

He changed to work clothes and boots. He came back out, ordered a few canned goods, and filled his canteen. Water wasn't going to be the problem it once had been, not with the Alamo running bankful with it.

"Charley, have my things moved over to the hotel. You'll be needing the room now."

He rode along the Alamo barranca, and it was a more pleasant ride than it had been because a man had the sight and sound of flowing water to take his mind off the heat. He tried to think of Amity as little as possible, but there was a desolate ache inside him. He swore at himself for the trend his thoughts were taking. He was quitting before he even made an effort. But he had played second fiddle to Hodges for too long, and maybe habit had grown too deep a root for him to uproot it. Besides, there was the certainty he had seen in her eyes. It wasn't Hodges' competition that handcuffed him so helplessly. It was the way she looked at him. But he'd try. He knew that. He'd see her just as often as she would let him.

The Alamo sometimes retained shallow pools well into the summer's heat. And where there was moisture, the arrow-weed grew thickly. Ordinarily they grew tall and straight, but now they were bending in the direction of the water flow.

He reached Hanlon's Heading and couldn't help but feel a quiet thrill of pride at his accomplishment. The river came through the gate and filled the Alamo, now called the Imperial Canal. It didn't matter what volume of water the river carried. The gate would control it, taking as much or as little as was needed. He had a right to his pride.

"Admiring your handiwork, son?"

He turned and grinned at Hall Hanlon. The old rancher could move like an Indian.

"Something like that."

"It's doing its job—so far. I told Hodges when he first looked at this, he could turn the valley green."

That was true. Mark had been with them when

Hanlon said, "There's your irrigation project. Two million acres of land, all of it laying below the river. Open her up, and in she'll come." Hanlon had had his own profit in mind, but Mark felt no resentment toward him for that. A man was entitled to all he could get. But his attention was focused on two words of Hanlon's.

"What do you mean 'so far'?"

Hanlon gazed out over the river. "The old lady's behaving right now. You ain't seen her when she's kicking up a fuss. Or sulking. She's a crafty, old witch, and don't you ever fool yourself you can relax for one minute around her. Because that's when she'll claw you. I've seen her in flood, and it'll make your hair rise. When the Gila River goes into flood and throws her load in with the Colorado's, a smart man runs."

Mark was aware of all that. That was why he had built the gate beyond Chaffey's specifications.

"But as contrary as she is a man falls in love with her. I've spent a lot of years around her, and I still don't know her."

Mark knew a little about him. They had split a bottle of whisky between them one night, and Hanlon had grown talkative. He had come into the desert as a young man because of his health, and the desert air had cured him. He was typical of the people who spend long stretches in the desert; lean and dried out with a wrinkled, leathery face.

Mark looked at the gate. "It'll hold." He intended it as no brag.

Hanlon surprised him. "I think it will, too. But she's got another punch she can throw at you."

"What's that?"

"Drought. I've seen her so low a mouse can cross without hardly wetting his feet. When the water loses its momentum, it don't carry the sand along with it. It can pile up and clog your canal. Every share of water stock Hodges sells binds him to furnish water to the farmers any time it's needed. What's he going to do then?"

Mark had prepared as well as he could for the contingency. With the flashboards removed, he could take every drop the river had. He had better remember to again mention those flashboards to Clell.

He smiled. "I think we can handle it."

Hanlon nodded, and they stood in companionable silence, watching the rush of the water.

Hanlon touched Mark's arm in a brief display of sentiment. "And I'm damned glad you're working for Hodges. It makes me feel better about—" He shook his head and let it die.

Mark wondered what he had in mind, then dismissed it.

"You'll stay for supper?" Hanlon's voice was gruff as though ashamed he had revealed a little of his inner feelings.

"Be glad to."

Before he left the river, Mark scrutinized the mouth of the canal. The rush of the water was scouring it clean. He couldn't see a place where the sand was building up. He could give his report to Hodges. He scowled at the whispering water. He knew Hodges hadn't been particularly interested in that report. Hodges could tell by the volume of water at Imperial that there was no obstruction here.

He grinned at Hanlon's questioning look. "I'm coming." Now he wished he knew what Hanlon had in mind to say about Hodges. He was building a composite picture in his head, and each man he talked to added a brush stroke. It was a disturbing thought, but the picture that was emerging was a far different one than the one he had carried for so long.

CHAPTER SEVEN

Mark stood in the doorway of the livery stable, watching Amity and Hodges until they grew small.

"They ride out a lot together." There was a certain slyness in Theobold's tone.

"Do they?" Mark tried to make his voice as blank as his face. Amity might not realize it, but she had made her choice. Only a blind man would fail to notice the way her eyes lit up whenever

Hodges was around. Mark felt more melancholia than rancor or bitterness. This was one of those fights a man lost before he got started. It was just a continuation of an old familiar pattern. He had never known a time that Clell Hodges didn't get what he wanted.

"It kinda bites you, doesn't it?" Theobold cackled with obscene mirth at Mark's expression.

"It doesn't bite me."

"Then what puts that poisoned-pup look on your face whenever you see them together?"

It was hard to keep anything hidden from those sharp, old eyes, and Mark tried to retaliate. "Old age must eat away a man's mind."

Theobold cackled again. "But it sure leaves him at peace with himself."

Mark wanted to say something about minding your own damned business. He turned on his heel, and Theobold's laughter followed him down the street.

How many times had he told himself the way to get her out of his system was to simply quit thinking of her. But she constantly crept into his thoughts. What he needed was work, hard, driving work that left room for nothing else. The water's arrival had taken away the need for that kind of work.

He walked to the edge of town, and stared somberly out across the desert. The ripples of sand showed the direction of last night's wind.

The wind was a tireless worker, building one day and tearing down the next.

Already on some patches the land was showing a faint mantling of green as the seed sprouted. Those patches belonged to the foresighted, ambitious men, the ones who hadn't sat around and quarreled about the delay in the water's arrival. They had gone ahead and cleared their land, and now the laggards fought and cursed the stubborn greasewood and envied the men who hadn't waited.

His mind picked up the problem of land clearing. There had to be a better, faster way than the slow, tedious method now in use.

He saw the slow-approaching wagon, coming from the north, as he wrestled at the problem of the greasewood. He supposed another settler was coming with high hopes of finding his Utopia. They came in a fairly steady stream, their eyes fired with a zeal to be on their land. A great many of them would know only relentless work followed by frustration and disappointment. He wondered why the bulk of men fell into that class. Some ingredient was missing in them, some element of luck. He smiled wryly at the all-inclusive word. At least, it gave the failures something to blame.

The wagon dipped out of view in a deep wash, and it took several moments before it reappeared. Details stood out more clearly when the wagon came back into view. It was an old and sorry wagon, with most of the good miles knocked out of it. Its right rear wheel canted drunkenly, and it squeaked and groaned. Its owner was the kind of man who had the cards stacked against him. He had little or nothing to start with.

Three people were in the wagon, a man and a woman on the seat, and a third person behind them, either sitting or kneeling in the wagon bed. The first two faces were old and tired, and Mark's attention went to the third. A girl, he thought, then revised that as the wagon drew nearer.

If she wasn't a woman, she was on the threshold of it. Maturity hadn't solidified the vague ouline of her face. There was no definite age at which maturity arrived. Mark had seen women at sixteen and girls of thirty-five. He would judge this one to be about eighteen. The mass of bright yellow hair was untidy, but that could be blamed on the desert wind. Her eyes were big and a startling blue. They stared back at him with unabashed interest. It was a pretty face, lacking definite lines to ever be anything more. The mouth was full, with more sullenness than humor, and Mark could imagine that generous lower lip could readily set in a pout.

She stood as the wagon stopped by Mark. This was no child. She had a ripe body, and the thin shift dress had little ability to conceal it. The wind molded the material to her thighs, and his eyes followed the sculpted lines. He realized he was staring and colored.

She wasn't offended. Her lips moved in a faint smile, and a sly, ancient wisdom was in her eyes. Women knew when they awakened interest in a male, and some of them openly showed their pleasure.

"Howdy." The man lowered the reins and nodded to Mark. He had a patient, weary face, the lines in it formed by a doggedness rather than determination. He had, the same blue eyes as the girl, but they were vague and unfocused. He sat slack-shouldered, and his overalls were too big for the thinly muscled frame. His big-knuckled, work-scarred hands were loose on the reins.

Mark smiled at him. "Hard trip?"

"Damned hard. Sometimes, I wonder if—"

"If you done the right thing coming here?" the woman sitting beside him finished for him. "Look at what you brought us to this time, Curt Newlin."

"Now Maud." While Newlin didn't actually cringe, the sense of it was there. "It ain't as bad as it looks."

"It couldn't be."

"My woman's worn out." Apology was in his sagging shoulders.

The girl tugged on his shoulder, and Newlin gave her a surprised glance. Then he understood. "My daughter, Letty."

91

Letty smiled at Mark. The smile was all woman, holding a bold brashness. Her youth and prettiness would create a stir of excitement in Imperial.

Mark returned the smile. "Mark Addison."

Newlin was proud of his daughter. "Would you believe her maw looked just like that not too long ago." The smile on his face was false. "Ain't that so, Maw?"

"Nobody would believe it." Her mouth tightened into a thin line. "You wore all the looks out of me."

His cringing was back. "Aw, Maw. It'll be different this time."

She was the type that was rough on a man. It showed in her tight lips, in the unforgiving eyes. Somewhere in the past Curt Newlin had stumbled, and Maud Newlin never let him regain his balance. It was hard to believe she had once been pretty. Her face was all sharp angles and sunken hollows. Her mouse-colored hair straggled across her forehead, and she made no attempt to brush it back. She had lost her feminine vanity and with it her spirit. She lived now to wreak her retribution from the man responsible.

Mark repressed his shudder. A man couldn't pick a worse hell than a vengeful, spiteful woman.

Letty's face was defiant. "It won't happen to me."

Maud Newlin slewed in her seat. "What won't happen to you?"

"I won't lose my looks."

Maud's laugh was loaded with malice. "I know what will happen to you. You'll take the first man who'll have you. You'll wind up with a passel of kids. Then we'll see where your looks go."

Letty's mouth set in a sulky pout.

This wasn't a new quarrel, Mark thought, only the continuation of an old one. All of them were caught in something not of their making and probably not of their picking. But once the vicious pattern gripped them, they fought one another instead of struggling together.

Newlin's expression grew more apologetic. "We're all worn out. It is good land, ain't it, Mr. Addison?"

"Good land. All it needed was water, and the water's here."

"See, Maud, I told you."

Maud stared straight ahead, not wanting to give him this small triumph.

"Where can I get my land, Mr. Addison?"

"Apply at the land office. Two blocks down on the right-hand side of the street."

Newlin nodded his thanks and shook up the team. The wagon creaked into motion. Letty turned her head to stare at Mark.

His eyes were thoughtful as he watched them. That family had known nothing but scarce times, and they weren't out of it by a long way. Newlin had days of work ahead just to get his land cleared. He might make it, if his money held out and his woman didn't tear him down too much. Mark wouldn't want his road.

One of McCaulley's freighters, Bill Shelby, lumbered toward him on his return trip to Flowing Well. Mark wouldn't want Shelby's job because of the sheer monotony of it. No sooner did Shelby deliver one load of supplies than he was back on the road after another.

Shelby gave him a big, good-natured grin and a wave as the wagon passed him. The monotony of his job didn't bother him. If he wasn't doing this, he would have to be doing something else.

Mark returned the wave and smiled. Maybe too much imagination wasn't always a blessing. It made a man restless.

"Damn," he said as the idea hit him. If a man could apply a heavy, long weight against those greasewood bushes, working on several instead of one at a time, wouldn't the clearing go that much faster? The answer had been before him all the time, and he had been too blind to see it.

"Bill. Hold up." He ran after the wagon.

Shelby braked to a stop. "Looks like something bit you all of a sudden, Mark."

"It did. I saw a pile of old steel rails under the water tank at Flowing Well. Are they still there?"

Shelby spit over the wheel and watched the

brown stream of tobacco juice furrow the dust. "Was the last time I looked."

"Bring me one back the next trip you make. Tell McCaulley I'll pay the freighting and whatever the rail costs."

"You plan on building a railroad with one rail?"

Mark grinned. "It's a start." He wouldn't say a word about his idea until he saw whether or not it worked. Jeers came soon enough without a man inviting them.

Shelby released the brake. "I'll bring her."

Mark turned toward the land office. Shelby thought he made a big joke about building a railroad, but if the rail worked, it would be as big a forward step as the valley would know.

Newlin came out of the office, as Mark reached it. His face looked stunned.

Mark took hold of his arm. "What's the trouble?"

"I ain't got enough money to pay the filing costs and get my water stock. And the man in there said, no credit."

That would be a clerk, but Hodges' return wouldn't change a thing. Hodges was even rougher about credit than the clerk.

Newlin popped his knuckles. "I ain't never had no luck."

Mark wanted to yell, goddamn it. Make some. But he held it. "Go see Bill Holt. His office is across the street from the bank. And don't go crawling in there. You stand up like a man and say you need a loan. Tell him you're willing to work like hell to repay it."

Newlin's shoulders lifted. "I always pay what I owe. Why are you doing this, mister?"

Mark wasn't sure. Maybe he wanted to help a family that needed it, or maybe he wanted to test his judgment against Holt's. Is it the girl, a sly voice asked. He yelled his "no" at the voice. Did he have to have a reason?

"Does it make any difference?"

Newlin's momentary spark of spirit was gone. "I guess not."

Newlin and Maud were quarreling as the wagon passed Mark. Or rather she was doing the quarreling and Newlin the listening. Letty gave Mark a blank-faced stare. Her lower lip was drooping. A girl had to have some kind of encouragement.

A week passed before Bill Shelby brought the rail. "McCaulley says you can have it. He's charging you for the freighting."

Mark nodded. If he had made a mistake, it wasn't going to be too expensive. "Will you take it out to the Newlins?"

"Show me the way."

Mark climbed up beside him. If everybody was as agreeable as Shelby, it would be a happier world. Of course, it wouldn't get a lot done, either.

Newlin's land lay four miles from town. Holt had backed him, and Newlin had hunted up Mark and poured out effusive thanks.

"Don't thank me." Mark had cut him off sharply. "Get that land cleared and show Holt you're worth backing."

"You watch me."

The evidence of Newlin's efforts were before Mark, but he had cleared a pitifully small area. At this rate the man would be weeks before he could even begin to think of planting. And Newlin hadn't been dawdling. He had put every daylight hour into it. It just took time.

Mark watched him chain a bush and slowly move the team forward until the slack was taken up. The muscles in the horses' bodies bunched as they threw their weight against the resisting greasewood. Then its roots gave way all at once, a tiny dust cloud puffed up into the sky, and another bush was torn free.

Newlin saw them as he turned the team around, and Mark waved him over.

Newlin's face was a dust-gray mask. His sweating had cut rivulets in it, and washings plus the dust obscured the overalls' original color. "I'm gettin' her, Mr. Addison."

Mark smiled to ease the man's visible anxiety. "I know you are, Curt. Maybe we've got something that might do it faster. Give us a hand."

The three of them put muscle into tugging the thousand pound rail out of the wagon bed. They let an end fall with a soft plop, and the puffing dust enveloped them.

Newlin's eyes were puzzled. "What's it for?"

"Split your team, Curt. Hitch one to each end of the rail. I think the rail's weight will yank out the greasewood."

"I only got one chain."

Mark made an impatient gesture. "Get a piece of rope." A rope would wear out by dragging against the ground, but it would last long enough to see if the idea was practical.

Shelby cocked his head. "It'll never work."

Mark gave him an angry glance. "You're smarter than the rest of us, Bill. We don't know until we try it."

He took one of the horses, Newlin the other. "Ho," he called and snapped the reins against the animal's rump.

It was an honest team, willing to work, and it took effort to get that rail started. The horses dug in their hoofs and slowly, the rail moved. Mark held his breath as it approached three of the greasewood bushes. It was going to hit all of them at the same time, and if it bounced over them, he was going to be sick.

But the rail was too heavy to bounce. The greasewood flattened before it, and their tough branches wedged against its edge. The rail moved ahead with no perceptible hesitation, and the bushes were torn out by the roots.

Mark let out his breath. Where the greasewood had been were barely discernible holes for the rail had dragged soil into them. He grinned at Newlin's ringing whoop. Newlin paused long enough to slap his hat against his thigh, unmindful of the dust it made. He had to do something to show his jubilation. Then he slapped the reins against horsehide.

The rail cleared a swath, its length, clear to the end of the field. They turned the animals and came back, and the results were the same.

"Do you know how long it would've taken me the old way, Mr. Addison?"

Mark knew. He wished Newlin owned all those rails at Flowing Well. He could have made some money out of them. Newlin wouldn't be able to sell just an idea. Other men could see its advantages in a few minutes of watching, and McCaulley owned the rails.

Shelby's eyes bulged. "By God, if that's not the slickest thing I ever saw. It jerks out the bushes and levels the ground at the same time."

That was true. The heavy rail flattened the hummocks, dragging them into the depressions. Massive valley planting was a lot closer than anybody realized.

Mark was ready to take another round, and Newlin shook his head. "You done more than enough for me already. I got some old reins. If'n I splice them onto these I can drive from the center of the rail."

Mark slapped him on the shoulder. This was the best sign he had seen. Newlin was beginning to think for himself.

Shelby climbed up to his seat. "You coming, Mark?"

"I'll walk in, Bill." He was too filled with the success of his idea. He wanted to stay and watch it awhile longer. Before much time passed other men would be here watching it. Shelby would spread the news all over town.

He helped Newlin splice his reins, and it worked fine. Newlin made a round, and it was as clean as the one he and Mark had made. At its finish he didn't even take time to exchange a few words. He was a driven man now, and he walked a little straighter.

Maud Newlin came out of the tent and stood beside Mark. She stared after Newlin, and Mark was surprised to see the mist of tears in her eyes. He had to lean toward her to catch her words.

"I know I jaw at him too much, Mr. Addison. But nothing ever went right for him. Maybe it's turned around."

"It's turned around." He stifled the impulse to tell her to back her man. Maybe she felt a little of it already.

Letty joined them, and her eyes were shining. "Won't you stay for supper, Mr. Addison?"

Out of the corner of his eye he saw Mrs. Newlin nodding approval, and he tried to make his regret sound real. "Some other time, Letty."

Maud touched his arm. "You will come again?"

"Sure." It was ridiculous that a girl's stare could make him this uncomfortable.

CHAPTER EIGHT

Hodges bore down on his pencil and broke the point. He swore and flung it across the room. Mark saw that wild, frustrated look on his face too often any more. He discreetly held his tongue. Hodges' wrath was always looking for something to vent itself on.

He knew what the trouble was. Hodges couldn't get his figures out of the red. On paper, the Company was taking in huge profits, for every share of water stock was being gobbled up by the steadily increasing flood of settlers. But out of the $8.75 a share brought, only a dollar of it was cash. The rest of it was on credit. Actually, each new colonist was a liability, for his stock guaranteed him irrigation within a specified time. The dollar cash, Hodges received, didn't go far against the expense of promotion, the digging of new canals, and the fixed overhead. Mark fully understood the position Hodges was in. He couldn't find too much sympathy for him. Hodges had wanted control of the Company. He had it.

"You need me for anything, Clell?" Maybe it would have been smarter to slip out of the door without asking, but he was getting a little weary of tiptoeing around Hodges' shadow.

Hodges lifted his head, and for a moment, his eyes were so wild he looked completely out of control.

Mark waited stony-faced. No more abuse, Clell, he thought.

Hodges' sigh sounded as though it were torn out of the very pit of him. His grin was close to the old one. "I guess not, Mark. These figures are driving me crazy."

Mark found sympathy. This was a phase. It would pass as soon as the Company's stumbling footsteps steadied. "I wish I could help, Clell."

Hodges made an impatient gesture. "You couldn't handle this."

Mark spun on his heel. The rebellion was back. Maybe he should show Hodges his diploma. He could add and subtract. He looked back, and Hodges' head was bent over the books again.

Mark smiled as he stepped outside. Perhaps he should be grateful to Hodges for his refusal of aid. Those books would tie him up for hours, and it gave Mark a chance to see Amity. Those chances were rare any more.

He walked into Ross's store, and Amity wasn't in sight. He didn't realize he was frowning. "Charley, where's Amity?"

"The ladies are doing something over at the church."

Mark's heart sank, and Ross's additional words sent it all the way down. "She won't be back all afternoon."

No wonder Hodges was putting in so much concentrated time in the office. He knew Amity was busy.

Ross scowled at Mark's expression. "Go over there and yank her out of it."

Mark grinned feebly. He could just picture all those weighing eyes, if he tried to take Amity away. And Amity wouldn't be pleased when she learned he had no concrete purpose. "I couldn't. I'd feel like an idiot."

Ross snorted, but he changed the subject. "Mark, is the Company in bad shape?"

Mark tried to hide his surprise. "Why, no." He hoped Ross didn't notice his hesitation. "We can sell more stock than we've got."

Ross's face was grim. "You'd better be pretty solid."

"What do you mean?"

"I think you're in for a fight. Congress just passed the Reclamation Act. Teddy Roosevelt wants to put the Imperial Valley under government control. I've heard reports government chemists are already here, looking for alkali."

"They won't have any trouble finding it."

Ross's face was sour. "Not even them. Don't you see what will happen? If they put out an adverse report, the settlers will quit coming in. If they can dry up Hodges' source of new money, can he stand it?"

Mark's expression answered him. "I thought so. If Hodges can be broken, it's wide open for the government to step in and take it over."

"Goddamn it, Charley. What's the government want it for? This country was built on free enterprise. Did you ever see an efficient government operation?"

"No." Ross made a weary gesture. "Power, Mark. The more a politician can control, the more it gives him. Don't you think for a minute the government wouldn't like to have everything in its hands. Does Clell know about this?"

Mark's eyes were troubled. "I don't know."

"Then you'd better tell him. He'd better watch every step."

Mark nodded and turned for the door. Hodges was burdened enough already. If he didn't know, Mark hated to be the man to tell him.

He stepped outside, and Bill Holt was coming down the street. Holt had a calm, able head. Maybe Ross was going off half-cocked.

"Bill, have you heard about this Reclamation Act?"

Holt nodded. "Where'd you get it?"

"Charley just told me."

"What else did he tell you?"

"That the government is trying to prove alkali in the valley. If they can prove nothing will grow here, the settlers will quit coming."

Holt nodded. "And the ones already here will panic and sell. Charley figures better than I thought he could."

"Do you think the government wants this valley?"

"I know damned well they do. And Hodges won't be able to stand up under their attack."

He grinned at Mark's swearing. "Maybe some of us can help Hodges. Maybe together we can put up a fight." He nodded abruptly and moved on.

Mark watched him a few moments in indecision, then turned toward the church. He had his concrete purpose. He wanted to talk to Amity about this.

She was coming out of the church as he reached it. The sight of her hit him hard, as it always did.

"Charley said you'd be tied up all afternoon."

She returned his smile. "We finished earlier than expected."

"It isn't too hot to go riding."

He thought she considered it before letting go of it.

"I wish I could, Mark. But I left so much work at the store."

He wondered if that were her real reason, and he managed to keep his wince hidden. "But I can walk you back?"

"I'd like that."

He grabbed for hope like a drowning man for straws. Her pace showed no hurry. Couldn't he consider that a good sign?

"It seems like yesterday since I arrived here, Mark."

And it seemed as though he had known her all his life. "I remember the day you arrived." How well he remembered it.

Her face softened. "So do I, Mark. I wasn't sure I was going to like it here. You taught me how to look at this country. Now I love it. I wouldn't believe it possible it could change so much in such a short time. Everything's green, and people are filled with hope. They come into the store, and I wish you could hear some of the estimates of what their first harvest will yield." Her laugh was gay and light, and he knew the familiar bruising of his heart. "You know, Mark, I believe them."

"I do too." He wondered if he should tell her about this new shadow that had fallen over the valley. He decided against it. She was too happy, and it was too precious to him to blight it.

It was amazing how short a distance it was between the church and store. He wanted to detain her, and he searched for something to say. How could he expect her to know how he felt? He had never said a word about it.

He drew a deep breath. "Amity—"

Perhaps she read something in his eyes, or the difference of his tone alerted her. "Mark, I've really got to run."

He caught her hand. This was the first time he had garnered enough courage, and he plowed ahead. "Not until I say something."

Suddenly she was distressed. "Please don't, Mark." She tugged her hand free. "Don't spoil everything." She whirled and ran into the store.

He could taste his sickness. This was irrevocable proof of all his suspicions. She didn't want to hear anything of this nature from him.

He grinned wryly, though he felt more like crying. He guessed that wrapped it all up and tied a knot in it that he couldn't undo. He turned and almost bumped into Hodges.

"Clell, I've got some information." He was too engrossed with what Ross and Holt had told him to notice the blackness on Hodges' face.

"What did you say to her?"

Mark blinked, then his ire rose. "That happens to be none of your business."

"The hell it isn't. You were trying to hold her against her will. I saw her jerk her hand free."

"Oh hell," Mark said wearily. He tried to stride by Hodges, and the heel of Hodges' palm jarred into his shoulder and slammed him back.

Hodges' mouth worked with his anger. "Don't you even try to talk to her again. If you do, I'll break your damned neck."

Mark glared at a stranger. Maybe an excess of things had pushed Hodges to this point, but Mark had a few things pushing him, too.

"Start breaking." He threw the blow on the echo of the words.

It was a good blow. It caught Hodges solidly and set him back a step.

Mark lowered his fists. A lot of things had pushed him, but now a lot of memories were restraining him. "You can stop it here, Clell."

Hodges shook his head. The dazed look was leaving his eyes. The imprint of Mark's knuckles showed vividly red on his cheekbone. That solid blow would have put down a lesser man.

Hodges' lips curled. "You'd like that, wouldn't you?" He came in cautiously, his eyes malevolent and narrowed.

Mark had less weight than Hodges, but he was sure he had more skill. But it would take time to wear him down, and he didn't want this fight to last that long. He backed before Hodges' boring in. "Clell, this doesn't make sense."

Hodges whipped in an awkward punch, and Mark slipped it over his shoulder. That was a powerful blow. If it had landed, he would have been down.

He was sorry for that first blow; he wished he could recall it. "Clell, stop it here."

Hodges' voice was low and ugly. "I'm going to beat your goddamned head off."

Mark's face hardened. "If that's the way you want it." He stabbed a left into Hodges' face and buried his right in his stomach. He was going to have to hurt Hodges to pound any reason into him, and he set to it. In the back of his mind was the dismal thought, this tears it wide open, this ends it. Hodges would never be able to overlook this.

He kept on the move, not letting Hodges plant himself. Very little time had gone by, but Hodges was gasping. Frustration was mixing with his anger, and his face showed he knew he was taking a licking. The gathering people knew it, too, and it was a silent crowd. This was the head of the Company battering itself to pieces, and it was a bad thing.

Mark stopped and let Hodges have his breather. He tried one more time. "How about it, Clell?"

"You'll never forget this," Hodges panted.

Mark's anger returned. He admitted he had started this, but Clell had laid a rough hand on him, and it was sufficient provocation. But he had also wanted to stop it a couple of times. That want was gone. He only wanted to finish it and get out of public view.

He moved forward, feinting and bobbing. Hodges' clubbing fist caught him on a shoulder, and it had a numbing impact. Mark grimaced. He was lucky Hodges didn't have any skill to go with his power. His own breathing had a tearing rasp, and there was a tremble in his legs. His shirt was plastered to his back. Fast movement under this sun put a harsh drain on a man.

He hit Hodges almost at will, driving him back across the walk. Mark gave him grudging admiration. The man could take punishment. He should have been down by now. He bled from a half-dozen cuts, and his eyes were glazed. His breathing was a hoarse wheezing, and his legs wobbled. But still, he tried to bull forward.

"Stop it," Amity screamed from the store's doorway.

Mark groaned at the sight of her. The only wonder was that the noise hadn't drawn her out here before. He could read the emotions on her face. The anger was for him, the concern for Hodges.

"Stop it," she cried again and started toward them.

Hodges' grunt had a note of triumph in it. It pulled Mark's attention back to him, and he was too late. Hodges had already started his charge, and Mark couldn't defend himself against it. Hodges' shoulder slammed into his chest and carried him into a wall. His head rocked back and smashed against the solid surface, and the force of it made his teeth ache. It turned his muscles flaccid and filled his eyes with water. He saw Hodges' blow coming, but he couldn't do a thing about it. It caught him full in the mouth, and he felt his lips break against his teeth.

Hodges' face was murderous. This was his only opportunity, and he took every advantage of it. His blows poured in over Mark's sagging defenses, and in a short space of time he would have beaten him senseless.

Only Amity saved him. She threw herself between them, using her slight weight recklessly. She yelled into Hodges' face and pushed at him with her hands. Something got through to him, for the insane light faded from his eyes. He stepped back, his face sullen.

Mark hung against the wall, fighting the waves of blackness that assailed him from the outside and the tide of nausea that attacked him inwardly.

He watched drops fall with fixed intensity, needing a focal point to cling to. It was funny about those drops. When they hit, they added to a growing red puddle.

He was bleeding, he realized suddenly. He raised a hand and winced as it touched his mouth. He looked at his hand and saw the bloody smear on it. He fumbled for and found his handkerchief. He held it to his mouth and raised his head.

The blackness was sullenly retreating, and his stomach was stopping its rolling.

Hodges had a nasty triumph in his face. "I had you whipped."

"You're a damned liar, and you know it."

Amity was now angry at both of them. "This is shameful."

"What could I do?" Hodges pleaded. "He hit me first."

She swung accusing eyes toward Mark.

"I did." If she wanted to make her judgment on Hodges' words, he would make no plea for himself.

Her eyes went uneasily back and forth between them. There was something more here, but she wasn't going to get it at the moment.

She sighed in exasperation. "Come on inside and let me get both of you cleaned up."

A stubborn pride firmed Mark's face. "Thanks. I can take care of myself."

Before he had taken his second step Hodges yelled, "You're fired."

It didn't surprise Mark at all; it didn't even break his stride.

CHAPTER NINE

Mark answered the knock on his door, "It's open," and went back to examining his reflection in the mirror. His bruises were showing up in livid splendor this morning.

Holt came into the hotel room, and Mark scowled at him through the mirror. "Don't give me any funny comments."

"Don't you always look this way?" Holt lounged on the bed, his face alive with humor.

Mark grinned despite himself. "I hope not. That wasn't a very smart thing yesterday, Bill." He hoped Holt would reoffer that job. He needed it now.

"But unavoidable, Mark. You and Hodges have been heading for a break for a long time. What set him off?"

Mark shook his head. He wasn't going to bring Amity's name into this.

"You busy this morning, Mark?"

Mark snorted. Holt knew damned well he wasn't. That was a piece of common knowledge, shared by everybody in town. Hodges had shouted his firing loud enough.

Holt stood. "I want you to come and see something. Might add to your education."

Mark nodded. Anything would be better than sitting in this hot hotel room.

He followed Holt into the lobby of the hotel and waited while Holt asked something of the desk clerk. The clerk pointed to a slim man just coming down the stairs.

Holt beckoned Mark over, and they waited at the foot of the stairs.

"Mr. Walton?"

The man acknowledged Holt's question with a slight movement of his head. He was dressed in field clothes, but he looked like a man playing at working. These clothes had seen little service. Field clothes in this country were sweat-stained and discolored.

"I'm William Holt. And this is my associate, Mr. Addison."

Walton's grip was firm enough, but his hand seemed cold. Like his eyes, Mark decided. Those eyes rarely blinked, and Mark wondered if the suspicion ever left them. He placed Walton in his early twenties. Walton radiated authority for his age.

"Are you in charge of the soil surveys?" Holt asked.

Walton nodded. "I'm with the Department of Agriculture." He shifted the small bag from one hand to the other. "If you gentlemen will excuse me—I'm late this morning."

"I was hoping you could help us," Holt mourned. "Mr. Addison and I are interested in buying a large tract of land. But we heard this land is useless."

Walton's eyes fired, and his hurry seemed to drop from him. "It is. Imperial is sitting on nothing but alkali. Before I'm through, I'll prove it's the same all over the valley."

"Have you told Mr. Hodges about this?"

Humiliation burned in Walton's face. "I tried to last night. I told him that selling this land to settlers was a fraud. He practically threw me out of his office."

That was Clell, Mark thought. He knew nothing about the subtle art of diplomacy. A zealot's gleam was in Walton's eyes, and he didn't have enough age or experience to temper it. Mark would bet that confrontation between Hodges and Walton had been something.

"You come with me today," Walton cried. "I'll save your money for you."

"We'd be grateful to you." Mark was sure Holt was grinning behind that somber mask.

They climbed into Walton's buggy, and the long-handled earth auger stuck out on both sides. The floor of the back seat was covered with small white stakes.

Walton unfolded a large map as he drove and handed it to Holt. "That's laid out in squares of seven hundred acres apiece. I'll take samples of the soil at the center of each plot."

Holt skeptically shook his head. "You can tell what the whole seven hundred acres are by taking one sample?"

Walton swept him with an angry glance. His "Yes" left no room for argument.

You're crazy, Mark thought. It would take a young fool to believe something like that.

Walton pointed out every glistening white patch of ground he saw. Each one put more triumph into his voice.

Sure, Mark agreed. Anybody would admit there was alkali around. But how about all the growing crops they passed. Walton never said a word about them. Fifteen thousand acres were under cultivation this summer, and the valley was green as far as the eye could see. On every hand sorghum, maize, wheat, barley, and alfalfa rippled in the stiff breeze; alfalfa as tall as a man's knee, barley that would reach to his Adam's apple. How was Walton going to explain those?

They stopped at Daigle's place first, and Holt introduced Walton. "Government man, Sam. He wants to test your soil."

Daigle's heavy, patient face was worried. "It's good land, isn't it, Mr. Walton?"

Walton pulled his bag from the buggy. "I can tell you that in a few minutes, Mr. Daigle. Bring a scythe with you."

He shouldered his auger, picked up a stake and his bag, and strode through a field of barley. Its heads brushed against his chest. "Clear me a space here, Mr. Daigle."

Daigle didn't mourn the destruction of this

beautiful spot of grain. He was too concerned about the remainder of his land. He laid the blade on with vigor, and Mark watched the tall stalks fall before its swath. His soul rebelled at the waste. How much land did this expert need cleared?

Walton waved Daigle aside. "That's enough." His face was grim as he started his boring.

Mark noticed he didn't sweat much. The exertion of twisting that handle under this sun should have brought out a lot of moisture, and the well-laundered shirt was almost as immaculate as when he started.

He bored five feet deep, then eight, and Mark thought, my God, is he going clear to China? Walton only stopped to add an extension to his handle, and his face grew more grim with each twist of the handle.

You goddamned fool, Mark raved. How much does it take to convince you?

Walton's face lit up as he extracted the auger again. "Hah! I told you." He pried off a slug of gray-white earth from the auger's bit.

Mark started to speak, and Holt's slight shake of the head stopped him.

Daigle didn't see it. "But that's eleven feet deep."

"It makes no difference if it's twenty feet deep. The land is ruined. You're doing all right this year. Five years from now you won't raise a thing."

He knelt, poured water from a canteen, and made a paste of the dirt. He measured its salt content with an electric battery, then estimated its hardness, friability, and percentage of loam. He drove in a number stake, then checked it on his map. It was the first time Mark had seen him look happy.

Walton straightened and gathered up his equipment. "I'm through here."

Holt's eyes gleamed in a grave face. "I guess you were right. The land's saturated with chemicals. I don't need to see any more. I'm hoping Sam will give us a ride back to town."

Daigle bobbed his head. His unhappiness was in direct proportion to Walton's happiness.

Walton waved as he drove off.

"The goddamned fool!" Mark exploded before Walton was hardly out of hearing.

Holt nodded. "Sure. But that's what we're fighting. He'll make his reports, and Washington will believe him, because it's the way Washington wants to believe. They'll thunder that Imperial Valley is doomed. The government wouldn't lie, would it?"

Daigle looked from one to the other, not following this talk at all.

"My land's no good?" He wanted a direct answer, something he could understand.

Holt's face was sympathetic. "I'll tell you how I'd figure, if this was my land, Sam. I'd say I got me a good crop this year, one that'll make me a nice piece of money. And there's no reason to believe it won't do the same the next and the one after. Hell, I'd figure on sitting on this land until my old age."

Daigle was still doubtful. "But his test—"

Holt's sharp gesture showed what he thought of the test. "Tell you what I'll do, Sam. I'll buy your land. Give you every penny you've got in it plus a decent profit for this year's crop."

Daigle blinked. "I'd—I'd have to think that over."

Holt shrugged. "It's a generous offer for worthless land. But the offer's open any time you want to take it. Now how about that lift to town?"

Daigle said little on the trip. Mark wanted to talk, but Holt was caught in an absorbed mood that discouraged it.

Mark waited until Daigle's wagon pulled away from them. "You meant that offer to him, didn't you?"

Holt nodded. "And I'm going to make a lot of them. Those tests are going to be the government's fight. It's damned little to hang a case on, but because the government says it a lot of people will believe it. It's a funny thing about a lie. Scream it loud and often enough, and people will believe it like the truth."

He pulled a cigar out of his pocket, cut off, and

moistened its end. "How'd you like to help me save this valley?"

Mark smiled. "From the government?"

Holt saw no humor in it. "From the government. This can be too damned fine a place for them to ruin. Hell, Mark, I'm offering you a job."

Last night, Mark had been certain he wasn't going to stay in the valley. But too much of him was in it. And there was Amity. He knew that door was locked, but he couldn't help hammering at it again.

Holt squinted shrewdly at him. "If I was picking a flaw in you, I'd say it was you don't carry a fight to the end. You let up a little, for one reason or another."

Mark started to flare, then held it. He might not like it, but it was a rational character analysis.

"You started the valley, Mark. Leave it when you know it can stand on its feet."

Mark stuck out his hand. "I accept. You'll have to lead me by the hand for a while."

Holt's pressure was firm. "I'm just damned glad you're with me." He chuckled softly. "You'll still be working for Hodges. Sure, you will. Hodges is ruined, if the new settlers don't keep coming. He has to have their deposit money to keep going. If we convince them this land is good, we save Hodges."

Mark grinned. "Even with that condition I'll take it."

"Sure, you will." Holt's tone lowered in warning. "Clell and Amity are coming down the street toward us."

Mark slowly turned, and his face felt stiff. He got a tremendous satisfaction out of the bruises on Hodges' face. What he did depended upon what they did.

Amity bobbed her head in greeting. "Hello, Mark. Mr. Holt."

Hodges stared straight ahead, his face wooden.

"Hello, Amity." Hodges had warned him against that. It was Hodges' move.

Hodges never opened his mouth. He was saying something to her, and she was replying spiritedly. If it wasn't a quarrel, it was on the verge of one.

Holt shook his head. "I never knew a female who didn't have a soft spot in her judgment. And they're usually too damned stubborn to admit it."

The words were like a big boot, effectively flattening Mark's ever-rising hopes.

CHAPTER TEN

The weeks it took Walton to finish his testing seemed like eons. Then he wouldn't state specifically what he had found.

Holt braced him in the hotel lobby before a bunch of men, and Walton's lips thinned. "I know who you are now, Mr. Holt. You've been working against me all the time. I know you've been telling the people my tests are meaningless." His voice rose as he addressed the dozen men in earshot. "Listen to him and be ruined. I've found dangerous alkali on fifty thousand acres and consider all the rest of the land to be under suspicion."

They crowded around him, begging to know which land held the dangerous alkali.

Walton smiled in cold satisfaction. "You can read the official report from Washington." He pushed through to the door. There he gave them a last pitying smile.

Mark was so furious he choked. One man had come in here and wrecked a lot of dreams. "You're harvesting bumper crops," he yelled. "Are you going to believe him?"

They paid no attention to him. They drew tighter together, their faces mirroring their worry as they discussed this.

Holt signaled to him and stepped outside. "They can't hear us now. All we can do is to wait for Washington's report."

"We should've ridden Walton out of town on a rail, Bill."

Holt chuckled. "I'd like to have held one end of it. But the army would've been in here tomorrow."

"What do we do then?"

"Wait." It was a cheerless answer. "Our biggest danger is panic before we see the report. If that

122

starts, it'll sweep everywhere." Holt swore softly. "The damned fools will sacrifice everything to save a little." He stared out across the desert, and there was sadness in his face. "This could have been so big, Mark. And man seems determined to smash it."

He dropped an arm across Mark's shoulders. "Come on. I'll buy a drink. Wipe the tears out of your eyes. We're not whipped yet."

For two months the tension of waiting for the report built until a man's nerves twanged under it. It was the damnedest situation Mark had ever witnessed. People harvested bumper crops in a daze, their dread of the coming report swallowing all other considerations. Holt said Hodges was going quietly crazy. At any moment the panic stampede could start, and it would roll him and wreck his dream. Mark speculated what it might be doing to Hodges' and Amity's relationship. Hodges was a difficult man under pressure. Whenever Mark saw them, he looked for some outward sign of stress between them. Each time he shook his head. He should know better than to even look for it. Stress would bring her closer to Hodges. She was that kind of a woman.

Holt found Mark at the livery stable. He had a small pamphlet in his hand. He riffled through the few pages of fine print. "This is what we've been waiting for."

Even old Theobold had new alacrity as he scrambled out of his chair.

Mark reached Holt first. "What's it say?"

Holt scratched his head. "I'm not sure I know. Most of it's too technical to be understood. And the rest isn't clear. Those people in Washington are either stupid or clever. They only sent a half-dozen copies. That gives rumor plenty of ground to grow on. Men will be clamoring for a look at it, and the ones who've seen it will pass it on in their own words. Each retelling will distort it more. I'd better call a meeting and explain it as best as I can."

The meeting was held in the street before the bank. Holt had no opposing voices, for men were anxious to catch every word.

He looked at the anxious faces and grinned. "If this wasn't so ridiculous, it would be funny." That struck no answering chord in those concerned faces. "We're harvesting bumper crops on land the government says is worthless."

"Read it, Bill," an impatient voice yelled.

"I'm going to. All except the technical part. I can't understand that, and I think I read as well as any man here."

That didn't draw even a chuckle. Mark saw Holt sigh. This crowd couldn't be kidded out of their mood.

"To boil it down to simple language, the report says one hundred and twenty-five thousand acres of this land have already been taken up by prospective settlers, many of whom talk of planting crops which it will be absolutely impossible to grow. Sixty-two percent of the land tested will grow most common crops; the rest is very doubtful. For the worst lands, the best thing to do will be to immediately abandon them."

"Which sixty-two percent is good?" a dozen voices yelled.

Holt shook his head. "That's the insidious thing about this damned report. It doesn't say. It lets each man sweat it out." He raised a hand to still the outburst. "I've got as much land as any of you. This thing isn't going to stampede me." He tossed the pamphlet into the air.

A dozen men sprang forward to catch it. One hand snatched it before the others.

Holt's eyes hardened as he watched it. "Use your common sense. You know what your land's been doing. You've got a choice. Believe your own eyes, or believe the report." He stepped down from his platform and joined Mark.

The crowd had broken up into small groups, and every voice was trying to express its opinion at once.

"I didn't do much good, did I, Mark. Maybe those people in Washington are clever. Which sixty-two percent is good? Is my farm among it?" He shook his head. "And the doubt will spread all up and down the line. What bank will lend a farmer money to buy seed when that farmer might be ruined in a few months? How can a newcomer tell what part of the valley to file in when any of it might be worthless? Watch for Washington's followup. This opening gun will be only a cap pistol."

At the moment, there wasn't a single constructive thought in Mark's head. He wished he could help Holt; he wanted to be a part of this fight. And right now, all he could think of was words—cuss words.

He turned at the timid hand plucking at his sleeve. Newlin's face was furrowed with anxiety. "Can I talk to you, Mark?"

"Curt, you know Bill Holt. Go ahead."

"All those words you said, Mr. Holt. Were you saying my land's no good?"

"Goddamn it, Curt—" Holt's restraining movement stopped him. He wasn't swearing at Newlin. It was just that he felt so damned helpless.

"You harvested a good crop, didn't you, Curt?"

Newlin nodded at Holt's question. "I don't know how many wagonloads I shipped off. A lot of Imperial ate my vegetables."

"Doesn't that answer your question?"

Newlin popped his knuckles. "I just don't know. I know I got alkali on my land. I've seen it."

"You don't try to plant there, do you?"

Newlin shook his head. "What I'm worrying about, are those patches going to spread and take over my whole farm?"

"I wouldn't give them another thought. You just go on planting."

Newlin's face was despondent. "I can't do anything else. Everything I got is tied up there." He turned and shuffled away, and his shoulders had the familiar droop.

Holt stared after him. "A lot of them will be asking me the same question, and I can't answer them any better. Those patches will spread. We know that. Damn Hodges for picking here to locate Imperial. It's the worst concentration of alkali in the valley."

"What do you want me to do, Bill?" Mark was drawing his pay, but he wasn't doing much to earn it.

"Talk it down. That's all I can think of now."

Mark stood there until Holt was out of sight. Holt's shoulders sagged, too.

The government took great pains to broadcast the report. Federal officials, all over the country, gave out interviews attacking Hodges and his Development Company. And they used the report as a basis for their authority. And the newspapers picked it up. Mark saw a half-dozen of the Los Angeles papers viciously exposing Hodges and his fraud. A short while ago they had been his most ardent backers. A bank in Imperial closed, and the Southern Pacific removed its construction gangs from the new branch line and announced the project abandoned.

Mark's anger increased with every passing minute. This was a great dream, already proven a highly feasible one, and yet men rushed to help stomp it to death.

He walked into Ross's store, and it was empty of customers. It occurred to him that every time he passed it this week it had been that way.

Ross grunted at Mark's greeting. "Mark, I'm selling out."

The abruptness of the announcement made Mark blink. "You're crazy, Charley." He kept his voice quiet.

"The hell I am. I haven't done enough business the last three days to pay to open the doors."

"You're going to lose a lot."

Ross's jaw jutted. "That's better than losing it all."

"I didn't think you'd quit this easy, Charley."

Ross choked. "Why, goddamn it, Mark—"

"The same thing you saw before that little government pipsqueak came is still here. Nothing's changed."

"You can talk that way. You've got nothing to lose."

"I wish I did have, Charley. I wish I had a fortune to put into it. I'd make myself four more fortunes. There's going to be a lot of people like you. A man will be able to pick up a bargain just about everywhere he looks."

Amity came out of the rear room, and Ross turned a wrathful face to her. "Did you hear this crazy man?"

"I heard him. Mark, will you walk me to the post office?"

She waited until they got outside. "Everybody's talking that way, Mark."

"I didn't think Charley would."

"He's scared," she flamed. "He sees everything slipping away—" She broke off and sighed. "I didn't think so, either."

They had a rare communion between them. Mark could add a third name to the list of stout ones—Amity Ross.

"Clell's going crazy, Mark. Every bit of his credit has dried up. And no new money is coming in. People are turning against him, blaming him for this."

"You don't blame him, Amity?"

"No. I know where the blame lies."

He had to know, and he put it into a blunt question. "You love him, don't you?"

"Yes." Her eyes remained steady.

It was odd how hard it clubbed him, particularly when he already knew it. He managed a twisted grin. "Maybe something will happen to change things." Whatever happened wouldn't make any difference—not to her. She would stick. What a practical joker life was. Any effort he made to save the valley saved Hodges.

He thrust out his hand. "You know I wish you all the luck, Amity."

Her eyes searched his face, and she didn't remove her hand immediately. "I know that, Mark."

He watched her walk away, and that numbed hollow swallowed him. She had slammed a door in his face with her definite "Yes," and its echo would never fade from his mind.

He went back to his hotel room and stretched out on the bed. He stared blankly at the ceiling, and his thoughts were a millstream, rushing nowhere.

He turned his head at the knock on the door. "Yes?"

"Can I come in, Mark?"

He sighed as he recognized Holt's voice. "Come on in."

Holt had a jubilant air about him. "I just left Amity, Mark. She told me what you said to Charley. That's the answer."

Mark stared at him. What had he said to Ross?

"Don't you understand? I've got a little money."

Mark grinned sourly. That was the understatement of the year.

"We'll buy whenever anybody wants to sell. We'll go out and look for buyers."

Mark heard him, but the words didn't make sense. Holt kept saying "we."

"We buy and buy and buy. Until my money runs out."

"I haven't any money."

Holt slashed with the edge of his palm. "Right now, that's not important. If we can weather the first rush, people are going to begin to believe we know something they don't. If that happens before we run out of money, it might stem the panic."

His excitement was infectious. "Bill, do you think they might even try to buy back?"

"That's what I'm betting on. And we'll sell back. At a little profit, Mark. Their lack of faith ought to cost them something. Get out of that bed and let's go out and spread the news."

Mark bounded to his feet. "You're the biggest gambler I ever knew."

Holt grinned. "I'll have to wait to know whether to cuss you, or love you. It's your idea."

They had no sooner stepped out of the hotel than a man rushed up to him. "Bill, you know that city lot you sold me a couple of months ago?"

Holt nodded.

"I'll take a thousand dollars for it. Eight hundred. Anything. Just so I can get enough cash to get out of here."

"You paid me eighteen hundred for it, didn't you?"

The man nodded.

"I'll give you a thousand dollars for it. Come around in the morning, and I'll have the money."

He took Mark's elbow and moved on, but his voice was loud enough to drift back. "That makes the tenth lot we've bought back today. We'll own this town before the week's out."

Holt's efforts to stem the tidal wave of panic that swept the valley seemed to have little effect at first. Every store had a FOR SALE sign in its window, and the vacant lots were plastered with them. Business was at a standstill in the town. Only the farmers went about their usual routine. They had to; the crops needed tending and irrigating. Besides, the majority had nobody to sell to and no place to go.

Mark met Ross on the street. "Still want to sell your store, Charley?"

"Why?"

"Because I'll buy it."

Ross spat into the dust. "That's what I've been hearing. You and Holt think you're pretty damned smart, don't you? You helped spread panic rumors around, then you buy cheap. You won't buy my store."

He spun on his heel, and indignation showed in every stride. Mark grinned. Charley had it all wrong, but it didn't make any difference. He would be another little rock to stand firm against the wash of the panic.

In a week, the tide began reversing itself. Mark heard whispers that all the rumors were a put-up job, managed by Bill Holt and Mark Addison. He heard they'd even had a hand in the government report. The thing that tickled him most was that he heard Hodges roaring at a crowd of listeners, "Those two are cleaning up. They're taking your money out of your pockets. Are you going to let them wind up owning the whole valley?"

The response took only a breath's length. Nobody could hoodwink them. "No," they thundered back at him.

Mark hurried to the hotel to tell Holt about it. Holt was talking to Downing, who had owned a hardware store. Downing fell silent at Mark's arrival, and Holt said, "Go ahead, Al."

Embarrassment stuck out all over Downing. "Bill, is there any chance to buy my business back?"

"Let's see. I gave you five thousand for it, didn't I? You can have it back for fifty-five hundred."

Downing's mouth sagged.

"I took a gamble. Don't you think I'm entitled to a little profit?"

Downing fumbled in his pocket. "I'm just tickled to get it back."

Holt grinned after Downing left. "They can't

stand the idea that somebody is getting ahead of them. Let's help that idea. Spread the rumor that prices are going up. That'll bring them running."

Mark spread the rumor. A word here, a few words there—the smart ones were getting back while the getting back was good. And each repurchaser added his belligerent belief to the growing bulwark of new faith. Nobody was going to chase them out of the valley and steal their money.

In less than a month, Mark couldn't find a FOR SALE sign anywhere in town. He pointed it out to Holt.

Holt nodded. "This may even be the seeding of a new boom."

"I wish Walton was here to see this. I wonder where he is."

"Poor Walton. He won't stand very high in government circles now. He was the reformer who failed. And yet in a way he was right."

Astounded, Mark stared at him.

"That old river has been pouring the bitter salts of sodium and calcium into its delta for millions of years. And in places the soil covering is damned thin. This is one of them. I think it's time to build a new town on a better part of the valley."

He walked on, his eyes absent, and Mark knew there was busy thought behind them. "Two towns, Mark. El Centro, south of Imperial. And

134

Brawley, north. We'll bypass Imperial and let the alkali have it."

Mark blew out his breath. Holt planned big, and Mark Addison was going to be part of it. And this time, he wouldn't have to beg for anything. Every time he looked at his bank balance, he was awed.

Another thought lodged in his mind. Curt Newlin's farm lay in the alkali that surrounded Imperial. He guessed the Newlins were his pet project, proof that an indigent family could prosper here.

"If you wanted to relocate, Bill, where would you pick?"

Holt didn't give it a thought. "Brawley. Right on the banks of the New River barranca. Lots of good land still open along there."

Mark turned off at Theobold's livery, and Holt checked him for a moment. "You figuring on telling the Newlins about it?"

"I thought I might."

Holt's eyes twinkled. "You've got a pair of pretty ears out there to listen to you."

For one of the few times in his life, Bill Holt was dead wrong.

CHAPTER ELEVEN

"Hold up, Charley," Mark called, as he saw Ross ahead of him. He caught up with him and pumped his hand. "I never see you any more."

"Whose fault is that? You never come around any more."

"Stop it, Charley. I've been busy."

He couldn't quite meet Ross's eyes. Both of them knew Amity was the reason he didn't come around. He saw her occasionally. He couldn't avoid it, living in the same town. He wasn't cured of her; he had only learned to adjust to it. Maybe he died too hard; it had been six months since she had told him she loved Hodges, and a faint hope that something would go wrong between them still flickered. He wondered why Hodges had waited so long without doing anything about her. The man wasn't this cautious in other matters.

"I thought since you'd gotten so big you didn't have time for poor people." Ross grinned and took the sting out of the words. He shook his head, as he looked up and down the street. "Who would believe it possible that Brawley could grow so fast? I'm glad I took your advice and moved my store here, Mark."

"El Centro's growing, too, Charley. But Brawley figures to outstrip it. It's closer to the rail outlet. It gets first choice of the settlers coming in. And even Walton couldn't find alkali around here."

Ross frowned. "But Clell wouldn't move the Company's headquarters here."

"That would be an admission of defeat, Charley. He picked Imperial in the first place. Imperial's dying, Charley."

He had ridden through Imperial a couple of weeks ago, and he had been shocked at the change. A few hard-heads, like Hodges, still hung on, but the town was reverting back to the desert.

"How does it feel to be an important man, Mark?"

Mark's stiffness vanished at the twinkle in Ross's eyes. "Not bad, Charley. It's a pretty good feeling to look at a town and know you helped build it."

Mark was well on his way to growing wealthy. Bill Holt was the reason. He had an eye for an investment and the money to put into it. Whatever he touched turned out well, and Mark participated in it.

Mark shook his head. "Holt's quite a man. You knew he talked the Southern Pacific into building a branch to Brawley, when I didn't think he had a chance. When it reaches here, watch Brawley grow."

The spur would be a profitable thing for both Brawley and the railroad. For this could be the garden spot for the entire country. The truck garden specialities of New England and the Middle West thrived here. Why shouldn't they? The sunshine was almost constant. All the crops needed was water and care, and the farmers gave them that. Even long-staple Egyptian cotton was doing well. And cantaloupes, tried on chance, were becoming the wonder crop of many thousand acres. All they needed was rapid shipping and icing. The Southern Pacific would supply the shipping, and Holt had already seen the need of icing. His new ice plant would be ready by the time the spur reached Brawley. Lettuce fields stretched for miles. Every imaginable food would grow here. For here, Nature was a benign companion. A farmer counted on two and three harvests a year and knew each would be a bumper one.

"You're lucky to be tied up with him instead of Hodges."

Mark knew that. There wasn't a man in the valley who wouldn't have traded places with him. Then why did this vague sense of dissatisfaction ride him? He was busy but restless. What he was doing wasn't his work. He couldn't explain it to anybody. They would look at him as though he was crazy.

He started to say something and held it. Letty was crossing the street toward them. Six months had made quite a change in her, too.

"Hello, Mark." She had a trick of putting a drawling inflection on his name. "Charley." That name was said in an entirely different tone.

Curt Newlin was beginning to prosper. It showed in Letty's clothes. She didn't have a great deal of style. She mixed colors with an Indian's abandonment, and the dress she was wearing wasn't right for her. She always approached Mark with an eagerness that embarrassed him.

"Letty." He set himself for the reproachful look he knew would follow.

"Mark, you didn't come by yesterday. And you promised. Curt waited all afternoon."

He was right about the look. My God, couldn't she be more circumspect when other people were present?

"I was busy, Letty. I'll try to get out there sometime tomorrow."

She gave him a sweep of her eyes, and something in them had dimmed. She moved away, and that was a relief.

Ross watched her recross the street. "She's turning into quite a woman."

Mark grunted.

"Are you in love with her?"

Mark's jaw sagged, then he blew up. "Goddamn it, Charley. She's a kid."

"You could have fooled me."

Mark's anger rose. "I met her family the day it arrived. If you could have seen them—broke and

139

hopeless. I was able to help them. Her father thinks I'm his good-luck piece. He won't take a step unless I advise him. He's prospered along with everybody else. And that's it."

He realized he was explaining too much. He expected to see derision in Ross's face, and instead, his eyes were shadowed.

"Sure, Mark."

The moment had turned suddenly strained, and Mark wanted to ease it. This was an old and valued friendship, and he hadn't worked at it very hard recently. "Have supper with me tonight, Charley." He didn't ask, but maybe Amity could join them.

Ross shook his head. "I wish I could. Prior plans."

"Sure, Charley." Was Ross's excuse genuine? Some wall was between them, and Mark couldn't understand its substance. He stood there until Ross turned the corner. It seemed that Ross was in a hell of a hurry to get away.

He sat at a window in the restaurant and ate a late supper, watching the traffic flow up and down the street. He returned a dozen gestures of greetings. He knew hundreds of people, and yet he was the most lonely of men. He made a sudden grimace. He was deep in the doldrums tonight; he was feeling sorry for himself.

He didn't want the rest of his meal, and he pushed it aside. The cook wasn't to blame; the fault lay with him.

He paused at the door to light a cigar, and Charley Ross came down the street. There was an aimlessness about his walk, and his steps weren't quite steady. Mark suddenly realized what it was. Charley was about half drunk.

He had no basis for his sudden anger at Ross, the turndown for supper wasn't sufficient reason, but he needed an excuse to vent his feelings, and he used this.

He stepped out in front of Ross. "Your prior plans must have been important ones. It looks like they came out of a bottle."

The words stung, for Ross flushed. "Don't take that tone with me."

The muscles along Mark's jaws bunched, then he forced himself into a semblance of calmness. Ross was in a quarrelsome mood, for he, too, sought flimsy excuses.

"What the hell's wrong with you, Charley?"

Ross thrust his face close to Mark's. "What's wrong with you? You let it happen."

Mark stared, dumfounded. He hadn't the slightest idea of what Ross was talking about.

He grinned and reached for Ross's arm. "I'll take you home and you can sleep it off."

Ross jerked his arm away. "Don't patronize me. Do you think I was lying about those prior plans. What would you say, if I told you I was attending an engagement party? I tried to drink enough to forget where I was, and the damned stuff

141

wouldn't take hold. Do you want me to tell you whose engagement party it was?"

Mark felt as though he stood in a block of ice that froze all physical and mental functions. Ross didn't have to tell him whose party it was.

"Hodges was here?" It was a foolish question, and he was sorry the moment it was out.

"With that cocky, know-it-all attitude twice as big as normal. Why shouldn't it be? He'd just picked off the biggest prize any man will ever get."

Mark didn't want that block of ice to melt, for when it did, pain would flood in. He thought of the happiness that would be in Amity's face, and the pain was starting.

"I couldn't stand it any longer. I had to get out before I said things I might regret." Ross shook his head. "Now I'm going to complete the job I started. Do you want to join me?"

"Yes." Mark reached for the arm again, and this time there was no resistance.

This whisky was sneaky tonight. For a while, it had no power to blot out Mark's thoughts. Instead, it sharpened them and brought them out into bolder relief. Then it dropped on him all at once, dulling the thoughts. But it had no power to dull the sense of loss. That remained deep inside, a sharp point of stabbing ache.

Their ways might be different, but each knew that loss. Ross turned ugly under it. "Your fault," he kept insisting. "You let him push you right out of the way. You didn't try."

Mark stared at him in outrage. All the trying was knocked out of a man when a woman said she loved another.

Ross started another string of accusations, and Mark slammed the table top with his fist. The bottle overturned, and liquor gurgled out to stream across the surface. "Shut up!" He glared at Ross's hot eyes.

An inner voice counseled, you'd better get out of here. If you don't, one of you is going to take a swing at the other.

He stood and lurched. He had to throw out a hand to a chair back to steady himself. He gathered what dignity he could muster. "You always were a damned fool, Charley. You never did know what you were talking about."

He turned and marched toward the door. He heard Ross cursing him, but he didn't look around.

He stepped outside and shook his head. The whisky was hitting him now. It pounded at him with massive blows that threatened to drive him to his knees. His hotel room seemed a million miles away, and he doubted he could make it.

He staggered into a hitching rail and leaned against it. Was Charley right? Could he have done more? "Old fool," he mumbled. "Never did know what he was talking about."

An arm went about his waist. "Come on, Mark. Let me help you." A tinkling laugh sounded in his ear. "I never saw you like this before."

He smelled perfume, and he peered into the face. "Amity?"

"It's Letty." The voice seemed to have flattened out. "I'll help you to your hotel."

He tried to throw off her arm, and he couldn't. He gave in out of weak weariness. She was a leech. To get rid of her, he would have to fight her.

He kept trying to seize a stabilizing thought, and they slithered away from him. "I drank too much."

"Yes." The word was clipped, the earlier amusement completely gone.

"Don't do it very often." He didn't realize he was leaning more and more on her, but she was breathing hard at the end of the block.

The hotel was in the middle of the next block, and the clerk's eyes widened as he saw the burdened Letty come through the door. He ran around the end of the desk to help her. "Is he hurt?"

"He's drunk. You can have him."

Letty turned to go, and Mark caught her arm. His thoughts were a deep, fuzzy wool, and every time he took a step into them, he sank over his head. She had helped him, and he was grateful. He tried to express it, and his tongue was thick, slurring his words.

"Amity, 'ppreciate this. Never can tell you—" She was glaring at him, and he couldn't understand it. It was hard for him to focus on her face, but she was furious with him. It rolled out in waves, and he felt it enveloping him.

The clerk took hold of his arm. "You need to lie down, Mr. Addison."

Mark stared forlornly after her as she walked toward the door.

The clerk tugged on his arm. "Come on, Mr. Addison."

CHAPTER TWELVE

In the morning, the clerk grinned at Mark's sheepishness. Mark shook his head. "I guess I made a damned fool of myself, Dan."

"You didn't cause any trouble, Mr. Addison."

Mark sorted through the mail Dan handed him. How well he remembered a pair of outraged eyes. "I guess I made Miss Ross pretty mad?"

Dan looked surprised. "I didn't see Miss Ross last night. Letty Newlin helped you here."

Mark groaned inwardly. His thoughts had been all mixed up, and somehow he had confused Letty with Amity. He wondered what he had said to her. He couldn't shrug it away.

"Thanks, Dan." He walked out of the hotel and turned toward the livery stable. He had promised to see Newlin. He could get that and his apology off his mind at once.

The attendant handed Mark his reins. "Getting dry, ain't it?"

It was an odd remark. It rarely rained in this country, and both of them knew it. "I hadn't noticed."

"Look at the irrigation ditches. I heard a dozen complaints a day that a man can't get enough water to take care of his crops."

Mark shrugged. That was Hodges' affair. A water shortage should be no problem. All Hodges had to do was to open the gates a little more.

He mounted and rode by Ross's store without the slightest desire to stop. That door had been closed pretty hard to him last night. He did wonder if Charley felt as bad as he did this morning.

Newlin was delighted to see him, and Mark grinned wanly. "Hello, Curt." It was easy to see Newlin's improved status. It showed in his equipment, in the better house. All the man had needed was a chance.

"Mark, what do you think about me putting in an orange grove?"

It had been proven that the trees would thrive here. "It'll take quite an investment, Curt. And time. It'll be six years before you can expect a return."

"Always wanted an orange grove, Mark. I can swing it. And I can wait."

It might be an excellent idea. Newlin's other crops would take care of him until the trees were ready to bear. And it would certainly put permanence into the future.

"Go ahead. Do you need any money?"

"I can handle it."

"Good." The first time Mark had seen the man he would have sworn the pride had been beaten from him. It wasn't so. He made his question very casual. "Is Letty around?"

"Letty," Newlin bawled. "Mark's here."

Letty came out of the house, and she was smiling.

He led her out of Newlin's hearing. "Was I pretty bad last night, Letty?"

Her eyes danced. "You were drunk, if that's what you mean."

He groaned. "What did I say? Was I out of line?"

"You got me mixed up with somebody else."

"That's all?"

She cut her eyes at him. "Amity Ross had a big party last night, didn't she?"

His eyes sharpened. If she knew about the party, she knew why it was held. Did that account for the difference in her?

He fidgeted under those mocking eyes. His imagination must be running away with him, but she seemed more sure of herself this morning.

"Well, if I did say something, I just wanted to apologize."

147

She took hold of his arm, and he felt the warmth of her hands through his sleeve. She didn't let go of his arm until he reached his horse.

"You'll come back soon, Mark?"

He looked down at her and nodded. It was the damnedest thing, but she seemed to have suddenly grown older. The unsureness he had seen in her so often was gone. The change improved her. She was a pretty woman. He didn't notice that he had changed girl to woman.

He nodded again and turned the horse. He didn't look back for quite a way. She was still there, and he raised his arm and waved. She waved back with enthusiasm.

He returned to town, and the first person he saw was Amity. He couldn't avoid stopping, for she had seen him. The radiance in her face left no doubt about her happiness.

"I'm glad for you, Amity." He made it ring almost true.

Her face sobered as she searched his face, then the radiance returned. "Oh, Mark. I'm so happy I could fly."

He had to sit here and watch that happiness when it was tearing him to pieces. How did a man make banal conversation when he was dying inside?

He was relieved when she said, "I've got to run, Mark. I've got a million things to do."

He watched the trim lines of her cross the street

and disappear around a corner. He jerked his horse around. The last glimpse of her made up his mind in a hurry. Brawley was the better town, but it wasn't for him—not with her in it. He had to find Holt and tell him he was moving to El Centro.

Holt was a wise man. He had looked at Mark's face and hadn't argued. "But build yourself a house, Mark. You can get a Mexican woman to clean and cook. Start living like a civilized man."

Mark had taken the advice. He built a four-room house with a screened-in veranda. It was far more room than he needed, but he liked the feeling of expansiveness. The Mexican woman he hired was old, but Mark wasn't after physical beauty. She had a rare knack in the kitchen, and that was all he was concerned about.

Teresina marveled over the cooler he made for the more perishable foods. It hung on the back wall of the kitchen, the three shelves in tiers canvas covered. A water bucket with holes punched in its bottom was suspended above it. The water dripped down, saturating the canvas, then fell into a pan on the floor. The pan had to be emptied frequently, but that was a minor inconvenience.

He had water piped into the house, and a tub installed, and people traipsed through the house to see this new marvel. Women looked at him with open longing. The tub alone made him the most eligible man in the valley. And still he was discontented. He knew what the true word for it was; it was loneliness.

Teresina nodded sagely at him one morning. "The house is too big for a single man. You need a woman to fill it."

He grinned sourly. "You're here."

A blush colored that ancient face. "Not an old woman. A young one that makes man hurry to get home. Señor, listen to me."

"Teresina, I haven't got time to even think of a woman."

She shook her head in disapproval. "Señor, you take time. It is not good for a life to be filled with nothing but work."

He was still smiling as he climbed into the new Studebaker wagon. It had been delivered last week from E. S. Bosbyshell of Los Angeles. He was the first in town with one, and he knew a pride in it.

He drove down the main street, and the town was thriving. It was amazing what had been accomplished in a few short months. And it wasn't like Imperial's beginning. This had the look of permanency. The street was lined with brick and frame buildings. Of course, the builders had the advantage of profiting by Imperial's mistakes. Holt claimed El Centro was going to catch up with and pass Brawley, but Mark doubted that. But El Centro was taking tremendous strides.

He stared unbelievingly. That was Letty just coming out of the bank, and she was about the last person in the world he expected to see.

He cut over to the walk, and the clatter of the wheels turned her head toward him.

"Mark," she cried, and her tone left no doubt how she felt about seeing him.

He propped up a boot and draped the reins across his knee. "What are you doing here?" He was idiotically glad to see her.

She dabbed at her forehead with a handkerchief. "Paw's second cousin arrived last week. He thinks he wants to settle around here. Paw drove him down to look over the land. I came with him. It gets so dull around Brawley."

"It gets dull around here, too, Letty."

She gave him a sweep of her eyes. "Does it, Mark?"

Each time he saw her, she seemed to have changed. She was quieter, and some of the rough angles seemed to have been polished. She still preferred flashy dresses, but with her youth she could wear them.

She touched a handkerchief to her cheeks. "They're in the bank, talking about money. It got so hot in there."

"I can offer you a drink of cool water. Better water than you've ever tasted in this valley."

Her eyes shone. "You'd better have a lot of it."

He stepped down to help her into the runabout.

She displayed quite a reach of leg above the high-topped shoe, and his heartbeat quickened. He picked up the reins. "I am glad to see you, Letty."

She squeezed his arm. She had changed. The child he had first known was gone.

Her color was high, her head lifted as he drove through town. She had never ridden in an outfit like this, and she drank deep of the moment.

He stopped before the house. "The drink first, Letty. Then I'll show you the house."

He dipped a glass of water and handed it to her. He was proud of the filter he had built to get water like this.

Her eyes widened, as she tasted it. "Mark! How did you get water like this?"

It was as clear as crystal, and none of the gritty element was left in it. He had bored holes in the bottom of an empty nail keg, then filled the keg to a depth of a quarter-inch with powdered charcoal. On top of that he had placed a layer of clean white sand. He had built up three such layers, and water filtering down through them came out of the holes clear and sparkling. The total cost had been twenty-five cents for the charcoal.

She listened attentively and exclaimed over his ingenuity. He was suddenly happy for no particular reason.

Teresina had been studying Letty, and she gave

Mark a nod of approval. "You stay for supper, señorita. I fix the best you have ever eaten."

Letty's expression asked the question of Mark.

He wanted her to stay. Somehow the house was different the moment she stepped into it. "Please, Letty."

Her words came in a rush. "Paw's not planning to go back until morning. I know it'd be all right with him."

Something inside him had picked up momentum, and he couldn't let it stop. He smiled at her. "It'll be all right." He wouldn't have it any other way.

Teresina did herself proud with the meal. The roast was succulent and tasty, and she illuminated the table with candlelight. Candlelight did amazing things to a woman's eyes. They put allure and mystery into them, and Mark stared more than he ate. Letty had a native wit that delighted him, and he laughed more than he had in months. He was startled to find how much time the meal took, and he was reluctant to see it end. A contrast formed in his mind: this house as it was now and as it would be in the morning.

He finally stood. "I'd better take you back now, Letty."

For a moment, he thought protest was in her face. She sighed, and her "yes" had a peculiar flatness.

She was silent until they reached the hotel. "Mark, I don't want to go back."

She came to him before he could decide whether or not he had reached for her. Her lips were sweet against his, then he felt a change in them. The change carried an ardent promise—if he wanted it.

He stared at the hotel entrance a long time after she had vanished into it. The future seemed empty without that promise. He thought he would be driving to Brawley very soon.

He was married within three weeks, and he wasn't quite sure how it had happened. It was a small wedding, just her parents and Holt attending. He carried her into the house, and the promise wasn't a lie.

CHAPTER THIRTEEN

He knew flights of wild happiness, but there was always a landing from them. Letty was as affectionate and capricious as a kitten. She gave lavishly in their intimate moments, but those few moments couldn't fill all a man's time. Between those moments, he found too much time to be critical. She had claws, too, and she displayed them, if she was balked in the slightest thing. She spent money recklessly, but that wasn't his objection. It was the junk she bought. The house was littered with it. And she flew into a rage, if she thought he was even questioning her purchases. She had replaced his comfortable, known furniture with ugly monstrosities. Even the bed hadn't escaped. He felt ridiculous every time he crawled into the canopied bed with its rows and rows of ruffled lace. She could quickly make him forget it, but afterwards, he had to lay there and look at it. He winced every time he thought of some of his friends seeing this thing.

He tried to give her the widest latitude in his thoughts, telling himself that she was young and she would change. She loved him. Wasn't that enough? But a sloppily kept house and poorly cooked meals argued against the question. And those things had a strong voice.

He still remembered his shock the first time he sat down to a meal she prepared. It had happened a week after they were married, and he had laid down his fork in disbelief. "Teresina must have been drunk when she fixed this."

Her eyes had turned cold and narrow. "I let her go, Mark."

He couldn't keep his voice from rising. "Why?"

"I couldn't stand to have her in the house, listening to everything we do. She did, Mark. I could see it in her eyes."

"Oh, my God."

She had burst into tears, and it had taken half of the night to pacify her. It wound up by him promising never to hurt her again.

He stepped into the house and looked about the living room with disgust. A patina of dust covered everything, and the floor hadn't been swept for a week. Last week's newspaper was strewn over the room, and sacks and boxes added to the clutter. Goddamn it, didn't she ever do anything but shop?

He stalked into the kitchen and swore. The pan, beneath the cooler, was overflowing, and water ran in a small stream across the floor.

"Letty!" he roared.

She answered from the bedroom, and he strode toward it. She lay on the bed in her chemise and slip, and her morning's purchases were scattered all about her.

She didn't notice his expression. "Oh, Mark. The New York Store had a sale this morning. Just think. I bought figured challie for five cents a yard. They almost gave away dimities and lawns. And fancy percales for only ten cents a yard. What do you think I paid for these shirting prints?"

The word "shirting" reminded him of something. It was as good a place to start as any. "Do you know I haven't had a clean shirt for a week?"

She stared at him, and her mouth trembled.

He noticed that weak emotion didn't reach to her eyes. "Don't start that." He was wound up tight, and nothing was going to stop him. "You bought the same junk last week. And the week before. Where in the hell are you going to put it?"

He watched her squeeze a tear out of her eye. She could call them up at will. "And get this house cleaned up. It looks like a pigsty."

The tears were coming faster. If he watched them, he would weaken. He stalked to a dresser and stuffed a change of clothing in a bag.

"Mark."

He turned reluctantly. She held out her arms to him. "Mark, don't you love me any more?"

She had the familiar club out, and he wasn't going to get close enough for her to use it.

"I meant what I said, Letty. I'll probably be gone for a couple of days."

"You never spend any time with me."

Her pout made him angrier, and he wanted to rush out of the room, but perhaps he owed her an explanation. "I heard from one of my farms this morning. The crops are dying for lack of water. I've got to go down there."

The pout increased, and his anger increased. She had no interest in any of his affairs. When he tried to talk about them, she stared at him with the blank disinterest of a child.

He kept his voice as calm as possible. "I know it doesn't mean anything to you, but where do you think the money you spend comes from?"

He doubted his control, if he said more, and he strode out of the room. Her wailed, "Mark" followed him.

His anger rode with him a long way before he lost it. This was the first time they had parted like this. He wasn't backing down. Everything he had said had been justified, but he could have handled it differently.

He drove past Sharp's gate, the gate that impounded the river water before distribution into the lateral canals. Nobody mentioned it often, but in its way, it was as important to the valley as Chaffey's. He noticed only a trickle ran over the spillway, and that diverted his thoughts. The season's heat increased daily. The valley needed much more water than this.

His farm manager was waiting for him. "Mark, they say they can't give us any more water."

"Who says it?"

"The *zanjeros*. When I ask for it, they just shrug."

"Have you talked to Hodges?"

"I thought you'd want to do that."

Mark didn't, but maybe he should. "How bad is it?"

"We've lost the lettuce. The alfalfa might last another two weeks. The other two farms are as bad off."

Mark dug a savage boot toe into the powdery soil. "I'll find out about it."

He started to climb back into the runabout, and a soft voice stopped. "Señor Addison. It is good to see you."

Genuine regard was in Mark's face as he gripped Tomás' hand. "Tomás, are you working here?"

"*Sí*. For the past two months."

"And you didn't let me know."

Tomás' smile didn't extend to his eyes. The eyes were sad. "I knew the señor had other things on his mind."

The sadness alerted Mark. Something bad had happened to make Tomás look like this. "Is Lupita all right?"

Tomás looked stricken at her name. "She is no longer with me. I knew from the first an old man could not hope to hold her."

The grief in Tomás' eyes sickened Mark. Tomás saw it and shook his head. "There is nothing anybody can say, señor. A man learns to adjust to what happens to him."

He shook Mark's hand again and walked away. His shoulders weren't as straight as Mark remembered them.

He swore in a steady stream as he left. The gentle people were always pushed around.

He let other matters erase Tomás from his mind. He wanted to drive to the Colorado River and see what was happening out there before he talked to Hodges.

Old, familiar scenes tugged at him. A lot of his life was tied up in this desert, and he missed the problems it posed.

He found only a workman at the Chaffey gate. He stared unbelievingly at the river. The bull was a weak, puny calf now.

"You think it's shallow now?" the workman asked. "You should have seen it before the weir was completed. Hell, it's twice as deep as it was. Those farmers will get their water."

The weir spanned the width of the river. It was formed of great sheaves of arrow-weed stalks, held together with baling wire, and laid end to end across the stream. The river had turned it into a dam, depositing the sand against the sheaves and anchoring them in place. The sand had continued to mount against the sheaves, plugging up the leaks. As the water level raised, it sluggishly began trickling over the gate sills.

The workman shook his head in admiration. "That Hodges is one smart engineer. This shuts up those squawking farmers. All of them talking about suing him."

It was a temporary expedient and no more. But the weir was probably permanent until the drought broke. With all those thousands of tons of sand anchoring it, it would hold until heavy rain fell in the mountains, putting the Gila River into flood.

The damned fool, Mark thought. Hodges had expended a great deal of time, labor, and money building that weir. Why hadn't he simply removed the flashboards and lowered the sills?

"He's created a new problem," Mark pointed out. "That sluggish water won't carry the sand. It'll silt up his intake canal."

The workman shrugged. "He'll have an answer to it."

Maybe, Mark thought, as he drove toward Imperial. His contracts promised adequate water at all times. Had Hodges, in desperation, been driven to grabbing the first solution that came into his head? Why in the hell hadn't he simply lowered those flashboards? Was it because Mark had installed them? Hodges might throw him out of his office, but Mark intended asking that question.

He walked into the Company's office, and there was no greeting in Hodges' face. "What the hell do you want?"

Mark had forgotten that there wasn't much forgiving in the man. "I've lost a lettuce crop."

Hodges snapped a pencil between his fingers. "I'd forgotten you're a farmer now. You'll get your damned water."

Mark leaned over the desk. "How long will it last?"

Hodges flared at the question. "I'll pay for the lettuce."

"I'm not here to collect anything. I was out to Chaffey's gate this morning. The water's not moving fast enough to carry the sand with it. That canal's going to silt up."

Hodges pounded his desk. "It's none of your affair."

"It is my affair. And everybody's in the valley. When that canal silts up, you'll think the first howls were just a weak whisper."

Animosity lay naked between them, and neither was aware that Amity entered the office. Her lips parted as she saw their anger.

"I built that gate, Clell. Built it to take care of emergencies like this. Didn't you want to remove the flashboards because I installed them?"

Hodges' suck of air was visible. His face paled, and his eyes shifted from Mark. "I—I don't know what you're talking about."

He was lying; it was written all over his face. He remembered Mark telling him. It was possible he could have forgotten until now. But Mark would concede no more.

Hodges saw Amity, and her presence increased the odd expression on his face. "I know why you didn't tell me about those flashboards. You hoped—"

Mark glared at him. "Go to hell."

He whirled and saw Amity. He was sorry she had witnessed any of this. He nodded as he passed her.

She followed him outside, and Hodges' roared, "Amity" didn't stop her.

Mark grinned wryly. Hodges was forgetting here, too. She had an independent mind.

"What was that about the flashboards, Mark?"

"I put them in to take care of drought, Amity. By removing them, the intake depth at the gate could be increased. I told him about them, Amity. If he chooses to deny it—" He let it drop.

She didn't comment, and he gave her grudging credit for loyalty.

"Amity, I know this. Desperation can muddy a man's thinking. But his thinking affects every person in the valley."

That drew a flash of fire. "Do you have the right to interfere any more, Mark?"

He gave her a bleak smile. "Yes. I'm one of those persons."

She stopped him as he started away. "Mark, I don't want a quarrel between us."

"Neither do I, Amity."

"I haven't even congratulated you on your wedding."

Somehow, he wished she hadn't said that. He gave her a gruff "thanks." Something on his mind had to be said, even though it might reopen the quarrel they both tried to avoid.

"Amity, I know you think it's only a personality clash between Clell and me; that neither of us will give a fraction. It goes far beyond that. What he does out at that river could lose or save us the valley. You've got the same stake as everybody else."

She looked at him with troubled eyes. "What are you trying to say, Mark?"

163

"That I'm going to watch everything he does. And if he goes wrong, I won't hesitate to call him loud and clear."

For an instant, her eyes heated, then they cleared and she nodded. "I can't see anything wrong with that." She had something else she wanted to say, and she held it.

He had a gnawing curiosity as to what it was. "I'm glad to have seen you again, Amity."

She searched his face, but she didn't speak. He looked back after a dozen strides, and she was still watching him. He wondered what was running through her mind. Surely, she didn't base his motives purely on jealousy. There was no longer any basis for that emotion.

CHAPTER FOURTEEN

Letty came into the bedroom just as Mark strapped his bag shut. He steeled himself for another ugly scene. She was angry. Her body quivered with it, but her voice was controlled enough. "You're going away again?"

He hadn't been home much in the last two months. She could rightly complain of neglect, but then so could his business. The struggle against the river engrossed him, and the fight was far from being over. He admitted it would go on without him, but he had to be there.

"Mark, how long will you be gone?"

Her plea softened his face. "I don't know, Letty." He moved to her and put his arms about her. For a moment, the stiffness in her held, then it melted against him.

"Mark, go in the morning."

He wasn't tempted, and that was a sad admission. "I can't, Letty."

She jerked from him, and her face flamed. The memory of other rejections was in her eyes. She couldn't understand how bone-weary a man could get.

"I've got to go, Letty. I've got to—" He stopped helplessly. He had tried to explain so many times, and she simply couldn't or wouldn't grasp it.

"Go! Who cares?" She ran from the room.

He could follow her; it wouldn't take much soothing to bring her back into his arms, but he shook his head. He had tried it before, and she always attempted to consolidate her minor victories into major ones. She would get over it; she always had before. That was a lie. At best, there was only an armed truce between them.

He drove through the business district, noting the amazing rate of building. He saw attorneys' and physicians' offices. There were barbers, blacksmiths, jewelers, photographers, contractors, and builders. El Centro had three banks and a grain and milling company. The new hotel was a handsome structure of two stories with a balcony, supported by heavy pillars, running all around the building.

All these concerns represented a heavy investment of money and faith in the valley's future. If the fight at the river was lost, all this was lost.

As he drove along the canal, he noticed that the water in it was low and sluggish. Hodges couldn't maintain a stable level. It raised and lowered, then repeated. And some of the distribution canals were silting.

The first person he saw at the river was Hall Hanlon. The river drew him with the same fascination it had for Mark.

"Mark!" He shook Mark's hand, and there was little greeting in voice or grip.

"More trouble, Hall?"

"It's coming."

Hanlon kept him well informed on what was going on. Hodges wouldn't give him the time of day. He had even tried to order Mark away, but he didn't own the land, and that left him helpless.

"His weir saved him for a while, Mark. Then he got that little flash flood on the Gila, and that helped him some more. But four miles of the main canal silted. If drought comes again, the valley won't get a drop." His voice took on a grudging note. "I'll say one thing. He's a fighter. He never leaves here any more. When one thing doesn't work, he comes up with another."

Mark nodded impatiently. Hodges was a trained

engineer. He wasn't doing anything out of the normal. "How's his new cut working?" Records showed that the Colorado usually dropped in the fall. Hodges had to remove those millions of tons of sand from the main canal, and the Company didn't own a dredge.

Hanlon shook his head. "I was against him cutting a new hole in the river. That old lady's mean, Mark. She lets a man think she's beaten, then she hits him good. He bypassed the gate and let a heavy current flow in during that short rise. He cut another hole at the lower end of the blocked section in the canal, put in a waste gate, and let most of the water flow out onto the delta."

Mark knew all that. It was a sound plan. The swift current would lift the sand and sluice it from the bottom of the canal, leaving it cleaner than before. Hodges intended closing both the bypass and waste gate after they were no longer needed. It had been working the last time Mark left here. But something had gone wrong. It was in Hanlon's face.

"The river dropped on him, and more sand than ever before came in. I told him that river was tricky." Hanlon couldn't help the gloomy note of triumph. "He cut the bypass wider, and that only let in more sand. Now he's in a hell of a mess."

"What's he doing now?"

"He hired the Bessie and wasted a couple of

weeks finding out she wasn't big enough for the job."

Mark nodded grimly. He could have told Hodges the little dredge couldn't begin to remove a portion of the sand.

"He's trying a new scheme this morning, Mark. He's been building a heavy boom of logs weighted down with iron. He says he'll stir up the sand and what water there is in the canal will carry it away."

"Oh, my God."

Hanlon nodded. "My feelings exactly."

The Bessie Cochan was already running up and down the canal when Mark and Hanlon reached the bank. She belched black smoke and churned up a huge wave. The sand rose in literal clouds, then settled back as the drag passed on.

Hodges was stomping along the bank, his face congested. "Faster. Get more steam on her."

"I'll blow her to pieces," the captain yelled back.

"Blow her." Hodges made a slashing motion with his hand, dismissing the Bessie and her captain. "I've got to get this sand out."

The increasing black smoke showed that the captain was trying. Mark didn't see how the boiler rivets held. Hour after hour, the Bessie made her four mile passage. Hundreds of Mexicans lined the bank, watching in awe. Mark shook his head. A little of the sand was being carried away, but the sluggish water let the bulk of it settle slowly back.

Hanlon guessed by Mark's expression. "It won't work?"

"No. But he'll keep at it until he tears her to pieces." Hodges' stubbornness would see to that.

"What are we going to do, Mark?" Hanlon wisely made it "we." It was everybody's fight now.

"I haven't the slightest goddamned idea."

September found the Colorado striking back in earnest. The blocked canal passed far less water than the farmers needed. Credit was getting tight, and Mark knew water rents must be far in arrears. Hodges faced ruin. But nobody got any consolation out of that. So did they. The fields were burning up. And the clamor grew louder and more vicious.

Mark faced ruin along with everybody else. Everything he had was in the valley. But that wasn't his chief anguish. It was the valley he wanted saved. He grinned wryly. In the saving of it, he would be saved, too.

He walked slowly downtown, thinking of the quarrel he had left behind him. That's all he and Letty did these days. To be honest, it wasn't all her fault. His nerves were stretched taut these days, and she seemed to love to pluck on them. The only peace he found any more was by leaving the house.

"Mark."

He turned, and Amity was hurrying toward him. He felt the same old flush of pleasure at seeing her. She and Hodges weren't married yet. He thought sardonically, with what Hodges had on his hands, he was in no position to think of marriage.

"Amity, I didn't expect to see you."

"I made a special trip, Mark. I know you've been worried about the river. Clell has his problem of more water for the valley solved. The telegram from the Mexican government came last night."

He frowned, not understanding this.

"He wrote them a month ago, asking permission to make a new cut into the river on the Mexican side. He's been going crazy waiting for an answer."

Mark immediately grasped what she was talking about. The Alamo barranca bent southward after leaving the river, crossing into Mexican soil. Hodges planned on making a new cut below the blocked canal. Water would flow in the Alamo again, but it could be at a high cost.

He didn't realize he gripped her arm until he saw the wince touch her face. When he removed his hand, the fingerprints stood out starkly white for a moment.

"I'm sorry, Amity. Did Clell talk about the kind of gate he was installing?" Hodges had a great deal of experience to draw on from the Chaffey gate. Surely, he wouldn't make another mistake.

She had a temper, and it showed life in her eyes. "You don't give him credit for anything, do you? You're questioning this?"

He scowled at her. "I'm not questioning his cut. That's almost a must. I'm questioning whether or not he's installing a gate at the same time."

Her temper faltered and faded. "I don't know. He didn't say anything about it."

He should have. He should have been filled with plans for it. Perhaps not telling her about it was only an oversight on his part. But it was odd that he would tell her one part and not the other.

"Where is he, Amity?"

"He went straight to the river. You're going out there, aren't you?"

He nodded.

She touched his hand. "Mark, if you see something wrong, handle it calmly, won't you?"

It was a hard request. Calmness was one commodity that was in short supply when he and Hodges faced each other. "I'll try."

He lingered, talking to her. Neither of them saw Letty standing on the opposite corner. She ducked back around it before Mark turned.

Returning home he called Letty's name, as he entered the house. He raced through it, and it was empty. He wanted to tell her where he was going, but a note would do just as well.

It was no trouble finding the site for the new cut. A dust pillar, towering into the air, directed him to it. The cut was being made four miles below Hanlon's, and Hodges had assembled a sizeable crew of men. The plows were already cutting into the bank of the river when Mark arrived.

Hodges nodded almost affably to Mark, and there was a new animation in his face. He was always this way when he had a new engineering problem to solve. He should never do anything else. It was only when the petty details of business bogged him down that his nature changed. Or it could be a hunger to be with his own kind that made Hodges agreeable.

"I've got it whipped, Mark," and for a moment Mark had the feeling it was as it used to be between them. "This cut will get the farmers off my back. My God, the screaming, the threats I've listened to."

Mark nodded in sympathy. "How big are you making the cut?"

"Sixty feet. We'll go straight west three thousand feet and intercept Imperial canal. The usual gradient will be enough."

Mark listened with attention. That should give Hodges the needed water. "What kind of a gate are you installing?"

Hodges pulled a sketch out of his pocket. It showed a wooden control gate that could be built cheaply and quickly. Mark noted with approval the specifications listed on the sketch. They seemed more than adequate. Hodges had learned from the Chaffey gate.

The gate should go in right after the cut into the river. With the water so low, now was an excellent time to install it. Mark's eyes wandered over the low, flat delta. The river roamed over it at will with scarcely any restraining banks. He saw where the Colorado had used a hundred paths through this delta already. It had a capricious mind of its own, changing its course on the slightest pretext. The slightest interference with it could make it change again. A bleak smile touched Mark's lips. He was endowing the river with the traits of a fickle and vindictive woman, and it wasn't too far wrong. Hodges' cut might be just the interference the river wanted. But his gate would afford protection. Mark shivered to think of what that river could do with that open cut without the gate to shut it off.

He watched the plows slice through the soft soil, and the little shiver touched him again. It was like opening the door of your home to somebody who had sworn to despoil it.

"When do you plan to start building your gate, Clell?"

Hodges' face turned evasive, and his eyes slid away from Mark's.

Mark's attention sharpened. "Tomorrow? The next day?"

Hodges forced a laugh. "Not quite that soon. I'm waiting for the Mexicans to approve the gate plans. I sent in the drawing along with my request for the cut. It'll be here any day. They must have overlooked sending it along with the permission to make the cut."

Mark felt as though he had been jolted with a hard blow to the midsection. He heard those words, but he couldn't believe them. A man couldn't predict this river's behavior for thirty minutes, but Hodges was trusting he would receive his gate approval before an emergency arose. This was pure fantasy, but Mark thought he heard ugly chuckling as the river slid along before him.

"Clell, are you crazy? You've seen this river rise in less than twenty-four hours. With an open cut, all of it could pour into the valley."

Hodges' eyes turned black at the criticism, but he managed to hold a semblance of control. "What else could I do but go ahead? In another couple of weeks, the valley would have been burned up. Lawsuits would have snowed me under. I've got time. I'll have the gate built before I need it."

Mark's voice shook. "And if you get a flash flood before then?"

There was a pleading in Hodges' face. "Mark, I've checked the records of the Gila River in

174

Yuma. In twenty-seven years, the Gila has never dumped more than one serious flash flood into the Colorado in any one winter. In some drought years there were no floods at all. As dry as the canals are, we can take one flood without any trouble."

Mark breathed hard. Hodges was gambling recklessly. Mark didn't give a damn what the records said. There was no law against them getting two floods this coming winter, or even more. The canals couldn't handle that.

Hodges was still pleading for understanding. "Mark, this serves two purposes. It gives the valley the water it needs immediately, and it proves to the Reclamation Service that we don't need American water. It'll get their hands off of my neck forever. This will force them into making a statement of policy. They'll have to give me the water rights for Imperial Valley. I won't be idle. I'll clear the old canal of its sand. Then I can jump two ways. Nobody will ever force me into a box again."

If Mark let the first word out, a torrent would follow, and all of them would be bitter and accusatory. It would end in violence, for Hodges wouldn't take it.

He stared hard at Hodges. "God help you, if you've guessed wrong." He wheeled and walked rapidly toward the runabout. Hodges shouted something he didn't catch. It didn't matter. It wouldn't be complimentary.

• • •

He walked into the house, and Letty faced him. She seemed slightly unsteady, and her eyes had a glassy glitter. He tried to put his arms about her, and she evaded him. He caught the fan of her breath as she turned her head from him.

He thought in astonishment, why she's been drinking. She often served wine with their evening meals, but this was far different. This was heavy drinking.

She retreated to a wall and leaned against it. Her dress looked as though she had slept in it, and she hadn't combed her hair. Looking at her was a shock. She seemed to have aged twenty years.

"What's wrong with you?" Distaste was plain on his face.

His expression drove her wild. "You think you've got me fooled, don't you?" she shouted. "I know what you've been doing. I know who you take with you on those trips."

He couldn't pass this off as liquor babbling. She was driving toward a definite purpose. "Letty, stop it."

Her laughter was harsh. "You don't want me to talk about her, do you?"

"I don't even know who you mean."

"You're a liar." She spat the words at him. "I'm talking about your precious Amity Ross."

He took an angry stride toward her. "You don't know what you're talking about."

"Oh, don't I? You've always been in love with her. I saw you pawing her on the street the other day right here in El Centro."

He thought back. That must have been the day Amity told him of Hodges' new plan. It was useless trying to explain to her.

"So you remember. And you thought I didn't see you."

His face was heavy with defeat. "Oh, for God's sake."

"You think I've been blind. I've known how you felt about her from the first. The night I helped you to your hotel, you called me her name. I thought I could make you forget her—" A sob rattled in her throat. "Now I don't care. Take her wherever you want to." She began to cry hysterically.

Anger engulfed him. He sprang forward and slapped her, and the blow's force snapped her head back against the wall.

She covered her cheek with her palm, and her eyes were insane.

The physical contact diluted his rage, and he was miserable. "Letty, I'm sorry."

"Don't ever touch me again." Her voice rose higher and higher. "You'll crawl when you want to come back to me. You'll see. I'll make you sorry. I'll make you beg—"

Any more talking would plunge her into hysteria. He whirled and strode out of the house.

Later, they might be able to talk. It might be possible to make something out of this mess, though right now, he didn't want to. All he wanted was to get as far from her as he could.

CHAPTER FIFTEEN

"Have you tried to see her?" Holt asked. He grinned at the heat in Mark's face. "Friend's privilege."

Mark sighed. "A half-dozen times. She went straight to her folks. She won't even talk to me. Maud's on her side. Curt doesn't know which way to turn."

Holt gave him a shrewd glance. "Do you?"

"No. If I beg her, she might come back. I'm sick of quarrels."

He wasn't sure he wanted her back on any terms. The house was empty, but at least, it was a peaceful loneliness.

"Everything turned sour all at once on me, Bill. I can't get my mind off of that damned open cut." Evidently, the Mexicans didn't send Hodges his approval, for the gate wasn't in. "Here it's almost Christmas, and the valley's been unprotected all this time."

"You're the only one worrying about it. People are claiming Hodges is a genius. Forget it."

Rebellion ran through Mark. Holt took it as

lightly as all the others. He softened the judgment. Holt was no engineer. He couldn't see the blade poised a few inches from their throats.

Mark spent a lonely Christmas and New Year's. The January winds sharpened, driving the rattlers and scorpions deep into their holes. The dry weather held, and the Colorado lay low and muddy. The Indians came down out of the mountains and danced their prayers for rain. And the dread lay in Mark's belly, gnawing away with sharp teeth.

He had been out to the Mexican bypass a half-dozen times, and there was no change—except that Hodges kept a gang of workmen out there. Evidently, he knew a little of that dread, for he had made preparations to close the bypass in a hurry. The workmen had driven a line of wooden piles into the sand across the canal mouth, then laid brush mats against the upstream side, weighting them down with bags of sand. The opening in the center of the canal had been narrowed down to thirty feet. Long timbers spanned it and were loaded with more bags of sand. Mark didn't talk to Hodges, but he knew what he had in mind. The timbers could be dynamited away, dropping the sandbags into the opening like a plug. Dynamite would do it suddenly, and the river would have no time to eat the dam away. It might work. Mark just didn't know. But the enormous amount of preparatory work showed Hodges' worry. It had taken tens of thousands of man-hours of work, and if Mark had to guess, he would say ten thousand bags filled with sand were lugged into place.

He was doing no good here except tearing himself to pieces. It looked as though Hodges was going to be lucky and not draw his flash flood. What Mark Addison should do was to take a vacation and forget the Colorado River.

He drove to Yuma and bought a shotgun and shells. Hiring a rowboat he drifted down the placid stream. The reddish water flowed sluggishly. But back in Mark's head was the sound the river could make when it stirred from its slumber. He swore at himself. As Holt said, he was the only one worrying about it.

He drifted with no purpose, nor direction. Occasionally, he shot a duck for supper, and nature did her best to soothe him. He was tired enough at night to sleep well, but the unanswered questions were only shoved to the back of his mind. Had he been fool enough to think he would find the solutions to Letty, to the river out here?

The Delta absorbed him. It was ever-changing, and each step brought some new facet of it into view. Nature used all its savagery in the Delta. It showed in the stunted trees, in the sun that was now comfortable but would turn cruel in a few short months. The wind was a constant force.

With the river as her tool, she had sculptured a thousand side channels and bayous, and each opened up a new world. A man could spend years here and never begin to know it all.

He was tired at the end of a day's tramping, and he wanted a hot meal and rest. His camp wasn't where he thought it should be, and he must have taken a wrong turn in this maze. He heard a sound in the distance that checked his breathing and widened his eyes. That was the noise of rushing water, pulling and sucking at the trees and brush as it pushed along. He forced his way through the last fringe, and the sight of the rampaging water froze him. The fading light gave the tumbling waters a reddish cast, and they stretched endlessly, covering the vast reaches of the mud flats. He could see his boat, still tied to a stump at least a half mile out in the flood. It was impossible to reach it in this ever-increasing torrent.

Even as he stared, the water rose and lapped around his boots. "The Gila's in flood. She's dumping this into the Colorado." He didn't realize he spoke aloud.

The water had a voice, a laughing roar of delight. Let men scan the records and depend upon percentages; the river didn't know how to figure.

He would have to make his way back to the canal on foot, and within a dozen yards he was running, fighting to keep panic from over-whelming him. He looked back as he ran. The water was rising with deadly swiftness, and it would be fatal, if a man injured himself and couldn't run. Other life was fleeing with him. Lizards and gophers passed him, driven from their holes by the rising waters.

He ran until his breathing burned his throat, and his legs shook with weariness. But he had gained on the water, and he threw himself down to rest. In ten minutes the water was lapping at him again.

He rose and plowed ahead, making wide detours around sandy depressions that had become lakes. Mesquite branches tore at his clothes, and he left pieces of them in its thorny grasp. It was after dark when he finally lay down, hoping for a few hours' rest. He was awakened by the cold touch of water. In the darkness he couldn't see it plainly, but he could hear it, and it was around him. He jumped to his feet and yelled, needing the relief of the sound of a human voice. He was grateful for a sense of direction, for it was all he had to guide him. He kept moving through the remainder of the night, and the water was always plucking at his heels. At times, he floundered through it calf deep. The mud dragged at his strength until his legs screamed at the forcing of the next step.

He was caught up in an endless nightmare of

fighting to increase the gap between himself and the water, and he was sure it would never end. It lasted through the next day and night, and he cursed the river until all passion against it was spent.

Early in the morning, he staggered through the last of the underbrush to the canal. It was running bankful, rushing toward the valley. But the dikes were between him and the river, and he could rest.

He fell into heavy but disturbed sleep, for the roar of the river kept pricking through his unconsciousness. He awakened heavy-eyed and drained. He had to warn Hodges of this flood. It was probably a useless gesture, for everybody within miles around surely knew of it.

He turned and plodded toward the Mexican bypass. He sighed with relief as he saw the adobe hut just ahead of him. The Mexican ranchero gave him cold, fried frijoles, tasteless but filling. The coffee was hot and strong enough to walk by itself.

The man listened to the river, as Mark ate. "It is a bad flood, señor."

"How long will it last?"

"*¿Quien sabe?*"

The expression and the shrug summed up well man's knowledge of the river.

He borrowed a mule from the ranchero and rode east toward the cut. It had been a long time since he had seen the canal carrying this volume of water. It couldn't handle much more without low sections of the valley being inundated.

When he reached the river, the main body of it rolled southward, so wide that he could scarcely see the far shore. He was afraid to look at the cut, fearing that Hodges' emergency pile dam had been torn out. But it was still there, and he stared in disbelief. A heavy sand bank had been deposited across the mouth of the canal, and the rushing waters were placing more sand across its mouth with every hour, further shoaling the intake. The Colorado smashed at Hodges with one hand and helped him with the other.

He found Hodges at a temporary camp, and fatigue had etched deep lines in his face. Hodges jerked up his head at the sight of him. "Where did you come from?"

"I got caught out there, Clell. I wasn't sure I was going to make it."

"It's been a hell of a couple of days, Mark."

How well Mark knew. "That sand bar saved you from having most of the river in your lap."

Maybe Hodges was too beaten to feel resentment at the remark. "I'm going to have to cut through that bar, or the farmers will be without water again." Before Mark could protest, he added, "I'll narrow the cut down. I can handle a narrower one, if I have to."

Mark wasn't sure of that. He had just seen

evidence of how viciously quick a Gila flood could be. The Gila came from the high, wooded mountains in Arizona, and the country tilted downward, sharply this way, giving the water tremendous momentum. But worse, it was loaded with trees and logs it had picked up in its mad rush. That had been no problem when the Chaffey gate had been in operation, for the trash booms, anchored before it, had warded off the bombardment. But Hodges' new cut had no such protection. If one of those trees ever got into the canal, it would rip out everything man built.

The arrow-weed, growing along the bank of the canal, was straightening. That meant the water was dropping almost as rapidly as it rose. The immediate danger was over.

Hodges' face was exultant. "I knew I picked the right place to make my cut. The river will throw up a bar every time there's a flood. I don't need a gate. The river will build me a natural one."

Aghast, Mark stared at him. Hodges had been shot full of luck to get by this far. He had no guarantee the river would build him another bar when he needed it. He had to go very slowly, he had to pick words that would make Hodges listen to him. "Clell, will you take some advice?"

That was a hated word to Hodges, and Mark saw the suspicious sharpening in his face. "Plug that cut just as fast as you can. You've been given one break. Don't sit and wait for another one.

That sand bar might not be there next time."

He knew he was lost before Hodges even started shaking his head. "I can't shut off all the valley's water." The suspicion had grown steadily in Hodges' eyes. "Do you want to see me ruined? Is that what you're after?"

"I say it's time to tell the farmers what you're up against. They believe in you. They'll listen. It's better that they lose a crop than to be under water. Plug this cut and get the Chaffey gate back in operation."

Color was mounting in Hodges' face. "There is no emergency. You saw how much water the canal handled. It can handle a lot more. I can waste most of it into the Salton Basin. Besides, there won't be another flood."

Mark's fists were balled. He had hoped there was still communication between them, but the last vestige of the hope was gone. There would only be communication as long as he agreed with everything Hodges said.

"You'd better pray to God you're right, Clell." He shook his head at the ferocious set of Hodges' face. He had just waved the red flag of criticism before him.

"Who needs your damned advice?" Hodges yelled after him.

CHAPTER SIXTEEN

Mark had to talk to Holt as quickly as he could, and he drove toward Brawley. He was within a mile of Newlins, and he debated before he turned toward the house. He hadn't done much about getting Letty to return, and he wasn't too anxious about it now. He grimaced. He was married. No matter how he twisted that around it came out the same.

The house was set close to the barranca's edge. Mark had argued against the site, but Newlin had wanted to be where he could look out and see the water. Newlin was in the yard, and he greeted Mark with warmth. He looked toward the house, and the warmth disappeared.

He was careful his voice had no carrying power. "Mark, I've been hoping you'd come by. Maud's sided with Letty. If I open my mouth, they both scream me down. Maybe you can talk some sense in their heads."

Mark swore. It sounded as if their attitude about this had hardened, and talking to them wasn't going to do any good. He looked at Newlin's anxious face and relented.

"I'll try, Curt. Letty's all wrong in this."

Newlin's sigh said he didn't doubt it. "You know how a woman can get a crazy idea in her head, Mark."

A new sound intruded upon Mark's thoughts. He threw a startled look at Newlin, then toward the canal. He knew that sound too well; that was the noise of rushing water.

"Is New River still running full?" It couldn't be. Hadn't he seen the flood subside? By now, the drop in the water had to reach this far.

"She sure is." No alarm showed in Newlin's face. All it meant to him was that his crops would have the water they needed.

Mark ran to the bank of the canal. The sight of the hurrying water had its fascination. New River was carrying as much water as he had ever seen it, far more than was needed for irrigation needs. Most of it would have to be wasted into the Salton Sink.

His tone took on new urgency. "How long has it been running full like this?"

Newlin gave it a moment's thought. "Not over a couple of hours. She ran bankful day before yesterday, then dropped to almost nothing. Then this morning she started coming up again."

The sun was shining, the temperature pleasantly high, but Mark felt a cold wind wrap about him. What he watched couldn't be happening, but there it was. It was against all records, it made a mockery of man's attempt at prediction, but there it was. The Gila was in flood again, right upon the heels of the first one. And he would say, bringing down even more water than the first time. He had to see Holt; he had to make somebody listen.

He whirled, and Newlin caught his sleeve. "Mark, have you forgotten about talking to Letty?"

Mark looked at that patient, enduring face and withheld his abrupt refusal. He was quite sure it would do no good, but he would try.

Maud appeared in the doorway before he reached it. A glance at her expression told him this was as far as he was going to go.

"Maud, I want to talk to Letty."

"She doesn't want to talk to you." She let a maudlin tear roll down her cheek. "My poor little girl."

He fought against his rising anger. "Maud, Letty made up all this in her head. I can guess at what she told you, and it doesn't hold a shred of truth." Letty was his wife. He could force his way in there and make her listen to him.

Then his anger was gone like a puff of smoke. Maud was determinedly planted before him, and it would take a struggle moving her out of the way.

He seized Maud's arm, and his fingers weren't gentle, but he wanted to be sure she paid attention. "Tell her she can come home any time she chooses."

He turned and walked to the runabout, shaking his head at Newlin as he passed him.

As he drove, he appeased his anger by thinking

he had done everything he could; short of crawling. He pushed it out of his mind. After he talked to Holt, he wasn't going to be the only man in the valley who was worried.

Holt's feet were up on his desk, and he looked at peace with the world. His lazy smile of greeting was swept off his face as he saw Mark's expression. "Something chasing you?"

Holt couldn't have hit it more accurately. The river was chasing him.

He saw the stubbornness form in Holt's face as he talked. Hodges' Mexican cut was a tiresome subject. But a new alertness dissipated the stubbornness as he kept on talking. "When I left, Bill, that sand bar was a natural barrier that kept most of the water out of the cut. But no guarantee comes with it. I'm not even sure it's there right now. If the river cuts it away and floods again, all of it will come pouring into the valley. Records show that the Gila floods only on the average of once a year. We've had two already, right on top of each other."

"You're not building something up, are you, Mark?"

Mark grinned painfully. "I make a habit of kidding myself."

Holt shook his head. "I never noticed it before. Maybe we'd better get out there and see what's happening."

Mark felt a wave of thankfulness. Maybe

190

Hodges would listen to Holt. If Mark thought Amity had any influence with Hodges, he would use her, if he could convince her he was right. He held onto it a moment before he let it slip away. In a way, if she listened to him, she would have to turn against Clell.

Holt looked about at the ripening fields of produce as they drove through them. "You'll never convince anybody else that things couldn't be better."

He said a final word of warning as they came within sight of Hodges' camp. "Don't lose your head, Mark."

Mark's first question was, "Did the sand bar hold, Clell?"

Hodges was eager to talk. "It's there, Mark. But it was a bigger flood than the first one."

"It showed. New River was running bankful."

Holt was more charitable. "Something bothering you, Clell?"

Mark expected to see Hodges angry, but instead he took a deep breath and went on. "Had a rough go of it, Bill. Look at the trash the flood brought down. It's almost blocked the canal. We had a hell of a time getting the dredge inside the canal and anchored to the bank. I was sure we were going to lose it."

The evidence of the struggle was in Hodges' face. He must have been a thoroughly frightened man.

"My God, Clell," Mark exploded as he saw the amount of trash that fouled the intake mouth. Holt's barely perceptible shake of the head stopped further outbreak. But Hodges walked a tightrope with no margin for error. He had to protect the valley from getting too much water and at the same time give it enough for irrigation.

Only a trickle of water was going into the canal. Another flood would plug the intake tight. Mark wanted it that way. Let the crops wither. That was better than the hungry water gulping up the land.

Mark couldn't keep the words bottled any longer. "Are you going to plug the cut now, Clell?"

Hodges looked at him as though he was crazy. "I'm going to clear out that trash and build a brush weir to the bar. That will raise the river's level and put more water in the canal. We've already had two floods. That's way above the average."

It took Holt's sharp, "Mark," to stop Mark this time. His easy grip on the situation never wavered. "Clell, how'd you like company for a while? We've got some time to kill, and we'd like to spend it here."

Hodges accepted reluctantly.

Holt talked to Mark after Hodges went to sleep that night. "I don't see what we can do out here, either, but I think we should hang around for a little."

Mark smoked in silence. He had accomplished one small thing. Holt took his words seriously now.

Holt made a final, wry observation. "At least, there'll be two of us to carry any warnings."

The late February days slipped easily away, and Mark and Hodges patched up a truce of sorts. Once, there had been a great bond between them, and part of it remained in their mutual love for the same work. The Colorado ran low, and the temperamental Gila was almost dry. Mark and Hodges experimented with brush and sand, piling a little here and a little there, off the canal mouth. Even a bucket of sand could change the pattern of the flowing water, and Hodges' fear gradually weakened.

"There won't be any more floods, Mark," he kept saying. This experimenting was gaining him knowledge of how to protect the intake mouth. The man's belief even bent Mark's thinking a little. Hodges could be right. If the floods were over for the year, and the averages said they were, Hodges would be given the thing he needed most—time. But the dread never entirely left Mark. He had seen how, too easily, the Colorado could throw itself about. If a single bucket of sand could change its pattern, no man could ever look at it with assurance. If this was his, he knew what he would do with it. He would plug that intake as fast as he could.

• • •

Hodges was openly exultant as the first of March brought no new floods. The water level in the river was steadily dropping, and he rushed his brush weir to reach to the sand bar.

With his eye, Holt measured the remaining distance to go with the weir. "He may make it through again." He shook his head. "Maybe he's one of the lucky ones. He skates on thin ice but never breaks through."

Mark gave him a wry grin. "I hope you're right." He wondered how much longer Holt was going to stay. He was surprised that he had stayed this long. But that river had a drawing power for all men.

Overhead, the sky was bright, but far to the east, high over the mountains, Mark thought a dark, sullen smudge lay against the horizon. "Bill, are those clouds in the sky?"

Holt looked in the direction Mark pointed. He stared a long time, shook his head to clear his eyes, and stared again.

"They could be. Now you've got me doing it. That's a long way off, Mark."

"The country tilts this way. If it's raining in the mountains, we'll get every drop of it."

The rushing tumble of water awakened him in the night. Branches and logs scraped and clacked against each other as they crashed together and tore apart. It was a long time until dawn, but he knew sleep was over this night. The Gila had struck again. It seemed to have a human intelligence, lulling them into false security before it smashed at them.

In the morning, he stared in awe. The Colorado carried a tremendous volume of water, probably more than the other two floods combined. Debris was piled high on the sand island, and more of it was whipping into the canal. Hodges' line of piling was taking a tremendous battering, and already here and there were gaps where some of the piling had been ripped out. With this rush of water, even if Hodges could dynamite and drop the plug, Mark doubted it would hold.

Hodges' lack of sleep showed in his haggard face. Anxiety was eating him to pieces. Mark saw the appeal in the look Hodges gave him, but at the moment, there was no compassion in him. That damned cut should have been plugged days ago.

There was nothing to do but watch, and the three men stood silent, their eyes fastened to the sweep of the waters. Then Hodges clutched Mark's arm. He didn't have to say anything; Mark had already seen it.

A huge oak tree rode the crest, looking as though it had been jerked out of the earth by the flood. Leaves still clung to its outflung branches, and its turning and bobbing put a snakelike life into its roots. Each man was frozen with some unknown terror. They didn't know what form it would take, but here was danger.

The tree struck the sand bar squarely, rolled over, and its crooked branches caught fast. It wedged too tightly for the current to move it on. The water pushed up against it, then spun off toward the western shore.

"Jesus." There was no irreverence in Mark's voice. A whirlpool was forming, and the size and power of it chilled a man's blood.

The eddies grew with appalling rapidity. They cut at the sand all around it, and they had the slicing power of a well-honed ax. The canal mouth widened before Mark's eyes, and more and more water poured into it. The whirlpool was cutting at the sides and bottom of the intake, and its centrifugal force was drawing the whole river in after it.

"Clell!" Mark yelled at him before reason returned to those haunted eyes. "We've got to dislodge that tree and break up that whirlpool."

Hodges' eyes remained dead. "How?" He seemed incapable of thinking at the moment.

"A box of dynamite will do it, if we can get out to the bar."

Mark had never known Hodges to lack courage, and he didn't lack it now. He caught Mark's thinking instantly, and new animation fired him. He broke into a run toward the work camp on higher ground.

Holt followed, protesting their madness every step of the way. He was still protesting when the dynamite was loaded into the Company row-boat. Mark looked back at him once, then the maddened waters claimed all his strength and attention. He knelt on the bottom of the boat and gripped the oars with Hodges. They had a navigational problem as well as the strength of the river to whip. Mark estimated the current to be traveling at seven feet a second. If they missed the island, they would either be caught in the whirlpool and slammed into the canal, or be carried toward the Gulf. Either choice erased a man's appetite.

He pulled until he was blinded by his exertion. A fiery band clamped around his chest, and he sucked flame into his lungs with every breath. They cut the long angle down toward the sand island, and their aim was true. Mark was just drawing his first relieved breath, when an eddy, at the nose of the island caught them. The boat traveled round and round in a dizzying circle, and Mark called for strength he didn't know he had to break the eddy's hold. He had no idea of how long the battle lasted. Surely, it couldn't have been less than an eternity.

Both men jumped out after the boat nosed into solid sand. Hodges started to throw himself down, and Mark yelled at him. He tugged on the boat, trying to drag it higher, and Hodges gave him a hand. They slumped to the sand only after they were sure the boat was high enough that the sand-cutting water couldn't reach it.

The fire remained in Mark's lungs for a long time. He couldn't remember when he had been so physically beat. He looked at his hands, and they were bleeding. And they had the return trip to make. He wouldn't let himself think about that now.

He grinned wanly at Hodges, as he stood. "We'd better get to work."

They moved cautiously around the lodged tree, trying to determine the best spot to put the dynamite. Mark wouldn't let pressure hurry him. They had one crack at this; it had to be right.

He stood in water up to his ankles, and he frowned at it. It should tell him something, and he couldn't quite grasp it. Then he knew. A few moments ago, the water had reached to his calves. The river was dropping, as fast as it had raised.

He had a hard time convincing Hodges of it. "The crest has passed, Clell." He broke off a piece of oak branch and thrust it into the sand at the water's edge. They intently watched it, and the river was falling fast enough for them to see the gap widening between water's edge and branch. They settled back onto the sand. In another hour, the water would be low enough for them to wade across.

"Goddamn you," Hodges yelled suddenly.

It startled Mark until he saw that it wasn't directed at him.

"It makes fools out of us," Hodges said bitterly. "Listen to it. You can hear it laughing." His face turned defiant. He wasn't ashamed of what he had said.

Hodges had no reason to be ashamed. "I hear it, Clell."

Hodges had been given another reprieve. But nothing had really changed. The oak tree was still lodged on the island, ready to funnel the next flood into the cut. Hodges couldn't be crazy enough to say there wouldn't be another one. Mark knew there would be. It was a feeling he had carried with him for a long time; it gained strength instead of losing it.

He decided not to say anything about it until they returned to Holt. If Hodges had any lingering stubbornness, maybe the two of them could make him listen to reason.

They waded across the channel, dragging the rowboat after them. Holt shook his head reprovingly. "That was a damned fool thing to do."

A bleak grin was on Mark's face. "Do you think we should've waited, Bill?"

Holt blinked. He looked back at the docile river, then at Mark. "Maybe we're lucky we've got any waiting time left. Clell, you're going to close the cut, aren't you?"

For an instant, argument flickered in Hodges' eyes. "Three floods in one season. Who would have believed it?"

Mark's voice was a great deal more composed than he was. "And the next one could finish us, Clell. We're going into the spring rise. We'll have a steady volume of water like we had a few hours ago."

It was hard watching a man making a decision that was killing him. Then Hodges sighed, and it was a weary, defeated sound. "I'll close it. But first I'll have to repair and strengthen my dam. I'll need more men, supplies, and—" His voice faltered.

"More what, Clell?" Holt asked quickly.

"Money." Hodges wouldn't look at him.

"Then we'd better get started on it. Do what you can here, Clell. Stuff will be rolling out to you in a few days."

Holt was absorbed in his thoughts as Mark drove away. "Mark, did this flooding put water into the Salton Sink?"

"You can bet on it. I wouldn't be surprised if the Southern Pacific tracks aren't already menaced."

"It could take a lot of money, couldn't it?"

"A hell of a lot. It depends whether or not Hodges closes that cut before the next flood hits."

Holt had an odd, little grin on his face. "Then I'd better go to where the money is."

CHAPTER SEVENTEEN

Mark's irritation mounted daily. Holt had been gone for two weeks, and he didn't have the slightest idea of where he was. He had sent loaded wagons rolling toward Hodges' work camp the first day he had returned from the Colorado, and he had hired additional workmen. He could do those things on just his signature, and it had made a noticeable dent in his bankroll. He hadn't gone back, himself. Perhaps there was more compassion in him than he suspected. This was Hodges' fight. Certainly, it was his doing that put him in it, but he deserved the opportunity to put the river back the way it was without interference. Of course, he had to have supplies and men, but the planning belonged all to him.

It left Mark nothing to do but to wait, and it pulled savagely at him. He could get no solid information from Hodges' camp. Now and then, he got a meager report from some workman who arrived in Brawley for additional supplies. The Gila had lashed out again shortly after the middle of March. Mark could tell by the rise in the Alamo. Now he wanted to know what damage it had done.

He checked his stride, as he saw one of the

work foremen across the street. "Mac," he yelled and ran toward him.

Mac was a sunburned man with big, callused hands and weariness dripping from every line. He returned Mark's greeting, and his teeth showed in a brief, mirthless grin.

"You want to know what the last flood did out there? I never saw so many damned logs come down that canal. We were afraid for a while they'd carry away Sharp's gate."

Sharp's was the impoundment gate on the Mexican border. If Sharp's went, there would be nothing between an open river and the valley.

"It carried away the plug Hodges intended dropping. Tore out every bit of his piling, before it lowered." He spat into the street. "A man works around that river enough, and he gets to hating it. It's like a damned Indian. It hits you a blow here, then sneaks around to hit you somewhere else. It's the total of all those little blows that wear you down."

Mark nodded in sympathy. How well he knew that feeling.

Mac's face was reflective. "I'll say one thing for Hodges. He never gives up. He's setting up a new dam. He thinks he's got a better way of building it."

Mark could find little enthusiasm for Hodges' stick-to-itiveness. Hodges was faced with something that never gave up, either.

"Anything you need, Mac?"

Mac's laugh was a short bark. "Enough time between floods to build a dam that will hold."

Mark touched his arm. "I hope you get it."

He watched Mac drive out of town, and a terrible restlessness seized him. He couldn't keep an ordinary business affair on his mind. The river had taken over all thoughts.

There was something he could do; he could see how the Salton Sink was handling the waste water. He seized upon it eagerly. It wouldn't be a long drive, and it was something with which to fill up these empty hours.

He drove out of the livery stable, and Amity was coming down the street. He stopped upon impulse. He needed companionship, and he hoped he could talk her into going with him.

Her eyes sobered after their first flash of welcome. "Mark, do you hear anything from Clell?"

So she had been left trying to fill the hours on her own. Don't you see, Amity, he thought. It will always be that way with him. Any problem that comes along will shove you out of his mind. He erased the treacherous thoughts. He was in no position to say them, let alone even think them.

"Just that he's still trying to close the cut. One flood after another has thwarted him."

"You're worried about it, aren't you, Mark?"

"Yes." He didn't amplify the terse word. "I'm

203

driving out to see how the Salton Basin is holding the waste water. Come with me. I'll have you back soon."

Her hesitation was brief. The waiting was harder on her, for she had nothing at all to do. She accepted this chance to be part of it even in a small way.

As he passed a corner two blocks down, he saw Maud Newlin. There was nasty knowledge stamped on her face. If he had had any hope of salvaging anything from his marriage, it was gone now. Curiously, he found he had few regrets.

He talked as he drove, sketching a picture of what the valley was up against. "So far, Clell has been lucky. The floods have subsided as quickly as they rose. But they poured a tremendous amount of water into the valley. If we get prolonged high water—" He let it stop, not wanting to put his fears into words.

"Could it mean the end of valley living, Mark?"

Those were the words he was afraid of, and he examined them soberly. Slowly he nodded. "It could."

He topped a rise in the desert, and the Salton Basin was spread out before him—but not as he remembered it. The last time he had seen it, it had been an arid, sunbaked depression. Now it was a sea. He had known a tremendous amount of water had rushed down the Alamo and New River barrancas, but his mind couldn't accept the magnitude of this. A mile out in the middle of that brassy sheet of water was the smokestack of the submerged Liverpool Salt Works.

He didn't look at Amity, but he was aware she was trembling. The sight of this would put a tremble in anybody. He remembered an evening around a campfire and an old man's soft words. "The sea will come again," Tomás had said. "If men's hearts are evil, it will come again and destroy everything he has built." The sea was here.

Far down in the desert, a train was waiting while a construction gang finished moving the tracks. Another flood and the tracks would have to be moved again. This was the main Southern Pacific's east and west line. The tracks could only be moved so far before they would have to be abandoned. The railroad, too, would be desperately anxious for the cut to be closed.

He sat there a long time, staring at that expanse of water. When he picked up the reins to turn back, the train was beginning to move.

Neither had much to say on the way back to Brawley. They had been given a frightening preview of what could happen, and they were held in its grip.

"Can he close it, Mark?"

He gave it studied consideration. Hodges had been close to success several times, only to have it whisked from him. It was almost as though the river was a human adversary, taunting Hodges with the hope of winning. He answered as honestly as he could. "I don't know, Amity."

He stopped before Charley Ross's store and started to say something. She stared wide-eyed past him. He turned his head, and Hodges stood in the doorway. His feelings were written all over his face. Mark heard Amity's faster breathing. He felt guilt, and that angered him. He had done nothing wrong, but he could appreciate Hodges' reaction.

Hodges came toward them, and there was threat in every line of him.

"Don't get any wrong ideas, Clell. I asked Amity to ride out and look at the Salton Basin. It's turned into a sea. The salt works is under, and the railroad has had to move their tracks."

Hodges' eyes accused him. They swept to her face and accused her, too. "Get out so I can break your neck."

Passersby were watching curiously, and it put color into Amity's face. "Stop it, Clell. I went with Mark so I could hear about you. You're acting like a child."

He stared at her in bitter outrage. "A child? I've been tearing my heart out for weeks. And the first chance I get to come in and see you I find you gone with him." He reached for Mark. "I said, get out of there."

Amity's eyes sparked. "I explained it to you. If you go ahead and start a fight now, I'll never speak to you again."

Hodges' lip curled. "He's lucky you protect him."

Mark felt the heat in his face. "I don't need—"

"Mark." The sharpness in her voice cut him short. "Don't make this any worse." She looked back at Hodges. "Mark's worried about the river. With all the trouble you have, it seems you'd welcome any help you could get."

Hodges paled under the criticism. Coming from her, it cut doubly deep. "Amity, are you taking his side?"

"Oh, Clell. I'm taking no side. Can't you see—"

"I know he's been trying to turn you against me. I can see he's succeeded." He leveled a finger at Mark. "Stay away from me. She won't always be around to save you. Next time—" The look on her face told him he was cutting his own throat, and he turned and plunged away.

Mark was afraid she would cry, then the trembling in her lips stopped. "I expected more from him." She sounded as though she had forgotten Mark was here.

"Don't blame him too much, Amity. He's been under tremendous strain."

She studied him with an odd intensity. "I wonder if he would be as charitable. I'm not sorry I went with you."

She was out of the runabout and gone before he could detain her. He suspected she would shed tears over this. His unwitting part in this didn't let him excuse himself. He shook his head and drove to the livery stable.

He came out and bumped into Holt. His anger had been contained too long, and it spilled over on Holt. "Where in the hell have you been? Was it easier to forget it by running off?"

Holt's grin never wavered. "I've been away on a little trip."

He let Mark's swearing build before he added, "To get two hundred thousand dollars for Hodges' fight against the river."

Mark gaped like a fool, but he couldn't help it.

"I went to San Francisco to see E. H. Harriman, the financier behind the Southern Pacific. I got to know him well while he was building the spur to Brawley. It wasn't hard to convince him how much the railroad stood to lose, if the river isn't stopped."

Mark drew a wavering breath. With that much money to throw into the fight, Hodges' chance of victory had ballooned.

"But Harriman doesn't think too much of Hodges. He thinks he's fumbled around too much already. He wants me to keep an eye on him. I don't know anything about that river. That means you have to be along. I need you to tell me what to tell Harriman."

"Clell and I almost came to blows a few moments ago." Briefly, Mark described the incident in the street. "I'm out, Bill. We wouldn't get along two seconds together. He's all wrong, but that doesn't make him believe it any the less."

"Why, damn his hardheadedness. I'll straighten him out in a hurry."

Mark shook his head. "It's his baby, Bill. I don't want a part of it any more."

Holt eyed him incredulously. "And you're the man who worried so much about it. Hell, I caught the fever from you."

"I still worry about it. But nobody's going to get anywhere starting out fighting. Clell's a good engineer. Give him his head and enough money and see what he can do."

"Do you think he can do it?"

Mark frowned. Everybody was asking him that question. "I don't know, Bill. I just don't know."

CHAPTER EIGHTEEN

Mark returned to El Centro and tried to occupy himself with business affairs. He gave them concentrated time, but the same quality wasn't in his thoughts. He had unwittingly caused Amity distress, and perhaps his complete withdrawal from Hodges' affairs was in the nature of atonement. He couldn't shut the river out of his mind. He kept the mental vow he made to Amity; he didn't go near it.

The spring freshet remained high. He could tell by the amount of water that flowed in the canals. And for an anxious thirty-six hours he had watched the water lapping at the top of the Sharp's gate. He could go there without too much fear of running into Hodges. After he had seen how high the water was, he couldn't tear himself away. It didn't seem possible that the gate had held against the tremendous water pressure. He told himself if it broke, somebody had to ride and warn the valley that it faced inundation. Then slowly, the water level dropped. He knew the flood crest had passed; the river was back at its cursed game of stringing men tight, of bringing them to the breaking point, then easing up on them. It left him feeling anticlimatic and more than slightly ridiculous.

For several days afterward, he had examined his inner feelings, trying to arrive at some kind of a conclusion. Had he magnified his dread in an unknown effort to give himself importance? Did he subconsciously want the river to destroy Hodges, hoping it would wipe out his standing with Amity? A lot of time had gone by, and no great calamity had happened. Yet he had been ready to cry wolf from the very first. He had been wrong, and Hodges had been right. He looked at it all as honestly as he could, and it told him nothing definite. Hodges was apparently without too much fear of the river, and he had too much. In retrospect, he would say the right man was handling the job. It wasn't an ego-bolstering conclusion, but he could live with it.

He saw Hall Hanlon in El Centro a month later and hurried to catch up with him. The old rancher looked drawn fine as though he had lived under strain for too long.

"Hall, I'm glad to see you."

Hanlon gave him a weary grin with his handshake. "Likewise. You've been making yourself scarce. We could've used you out there."

Mark made no attempt to explain his absence. "You've had a lot of high water. I've been watching the canals."

"It's a high-water year, and they don't come one at a time. I'll bet she'll really go up next year."

Mark laughed. "That's too far off to worry about."

"You'd better start worrying about it. It'll probably all be dumped in your laps."

Mark felt the familiar clutch of dread. "Hasn't Hodges closed that cut yet?"

Hanlon ran his tongue around the inside of his mouth and spat into the dust. "Personally, I don't think he ever will close it. He ain't the man for the job. And that river's got a hate for him. He was the first man who tampered with her. She's never going to forgive him for it."

Here was Mark's opportunity to get firsthand information as to what was happening out there. Everything in the past few weeks had been fragments he had picked up from some traveler, or from a few lines in the newspapers, and neither source knew too well what they talked about.

He took hold of Hanlon's arm. "Hall, I'll buy a drink."

"And I'll take it."

Mark waited until Hanlon finished part of his drink. "What's happening out there, Hall?"

"Why don't you come back, Mark? We need some brains out there."

Mark shook his head. "Clell and I don't get along." The explanation was too personal to make.

"He doesn't get along with anybody. He's wrangling with the engineers the railroad sent out to help him. The trouble with him is that he has to do everything himself. And the job's been too big for that from the start."

If the railroad had sent engineers, that meant Hodges had run into trouble. The core of dread in Mark picked up a new coldness. "What happened, Hall?"

Hanlon's face twisted. "You haven't heard? It's worse than it was before. Hodges was waiting for the water to go down so he could finish his pile dam and close the cut. Some riffle of sand or something deflected the currect directly off the canal mouth. Who knows what it takes to set the Colorado off? It built into a whirlpool, and I stood there and watched it grow. It swung across the west channel and began to chew away at the lower bank of the canal. It carried sand around in a circle and deposited it all around the rim."

Mark's face was absorbed. He could see it as plainly as though he had been there himself. He didn't know what had happened, but he could feel the menace of it.

Hanlon finished his drink. "Before the day was out, it built a dam from the sand bar to the mouth of the canal, and the western half of the river was pouring into the canal. Then the old lady really got to work. Confined in the narrow canal it speeded up and gouged the sand from the bottom. It didn't take it long to turn the mouth of the bypass into a narrow crevasse, a lot deeper than the surrounding river bottom. Then it began to cut that crevasse back upstream. It cut past the island and out into the main body of the river. I swear I could hear the river chuckling as it poured into the gouge it had cut."

Mark let out an explosive breath. "My God, Hall. Then it's open for the entire river. If it wasn't low water, we'd be under now."

Hanlon grunted. "Not so low. When I left about forty thousand cubic feet per second was pouring in. Think of what will happen, if we get a sudden rise."

Mark was. Hodges had a new problem, a far more serious one. No longer could he plug the cut and shut off the danger. Now he had to lift the Colorado bodily out of its new crevasse and set it down on the Arizona side, then build a dike to keep it there.

"What's he doing?"

Hanlon's face was gloomy. "It won't be enough. It never is. He tried to build a dam straight across the channel, stop the river and force it to rise until it reached the old level. Maybe then it would flow naturally to the Gulf."

Mark saw the picture. No mere brush weir would do it. This would have to be something strong to withstand feet and feet of water pressure. It would be a tremendous engineering problem.

"How did he do, Hall?"

Hanlon signaled for another drink. "You know the confidence he throws at things. He planned to make it stout. He ordered a floating pile driver sent down by the railroad from Yuma. Piles of logs and big reels of barbed wire were shipped in by barge and unloaded on the island. He hired every Mexican and Indian he could find. If he got his piles down, he intended to face them with a heavy blanket of brush interwoven with barbed wire. If it worked, the river would build up a sand bar against it and shut itself off."

Mark was absorbed in Hanlon's graphic

description. But there had been too many "ifs" in it. He hated to say what he knew. "He didn't make it?"

Hanlon breathed out a heavy sigh. "No man could've tried harder. He risked his life a dozen times a day. And he came close. But he had to build a dam more than a half-mile long. Setting every pile in that current was a struggle, and it took more struggle to lace the wire and brush between them. They got almost across, and his woven mat was trapping the sand, forcing the river to rise to its former level. But as the opening narrowed, the current got stronger. It yanked the piles out as fast as he got them in. It picked up a ninety-foot log as easily as you'd pick up a toothpick. He finally lost a man. Dragged along the river bottom at the end of a cable. I guess it took the heart out of Hodges. He abandoned that plan. Sixty thousand dollars poured into the river with nothing to show for it."

"And that's the way it was left?"

"Yep. Except that the railroad sent down more engineers to see what to do about it. They were wrangling about what to do when I left for El Centro."

Mark had lived every step of that fight as Hanlon related it. But futility was Hodges only gain. The valley was at the mercy of the river. The first rise would send enough water to wipe out the farms. If anything, Hodges had probably given

215

the river a sharper tool. It now had a wider, deeper channel to pour into the valley.

"Come back with me. They need all the brains they can get out there. You may see something that might be the key they need." Hanlon saw the refusal in Mark's face before he voiced it. "Don't say it isn't your fight. Before this is over, everybody is going to be in it up to his neck."

"It's a personal quarrel, Hall. Clell wouldn't let me near the job."

Hanlon's face heated. "I hope to God before long he doesn't have anything to say about it. Thanks for the drinks. I guess I got to be getting back." He stood and moved wearily toward the door.

Mark's face was brooding. A lot of people would shrug off Hanlon's words as those of a crazy, old prophet. But when Hanlon made a prediction about the river, it was based on long experience with it. Mark had sworn he would take himself out of this fight, and even if he changed his mind, what could he do about it? But he could do one thing; he could drive to Brawley and get Holt's opinion. Holt was the link between Hodges and the railroad's money. Mark wanted to find out how strong that link was. For what money Hodges had left wouldn't be enough, not nearly enough.

He headed north, noticing that the September sun seemed to be losing a little of its fierce kick.

It came as a shock to realize that this much of the year was gone. And all that had been accomplished was to open the door a little wider to the river. If Hodges got another fall and winter like the last, he was doomed. But maybe luck would turn for him, and he wouldn't get the Gila's flash floods. But he still faced next spring's rise, and that was almost inevitable. Spring wasn't too far away, not for the job Hodges had to whip. Mark shivered for no accountable reason. He didn't see how Hodges kept his sanity.

CHAPTER NINETEEN

Mark asked at Holt's bank in Brawley where he could find him. Nielson, his cashier, shook his head in exasperation. He was a thin man with a sallow, peaked face with an interest only in figures.

"He should be back before the week is out, Mark. He spends all his time at the river now. I never see him long enough to even begin to discuss important matters."

"You don't think the river is important?"

"Of course it's important. But there are other things more pressing. The river is—" Nielson hunted for the right words.

"So far away," Mark finished for him.

Nielson flushed. "For months everybody's been

listening to the river's danger. Has anything happened? Yet the pessimists advised long ago to make plans to abandon the valley."

Mark smiled. "I was one of those early pessimists, wasn't I, Karl? Think of all the crops that would have been abandoned, all the money lost, if anybody had listened to me."

Nielson ducked his head. "I wasn't blaming you. It's just—"

"That nothing's happened." Mark finished another sentence for him. "Tell Bill I'm in town."

Mark understood Nielson's attitude. When people lived with repeated cries of danger, all of its scare effect was lost. Not because the danger was removed, but because the repetition of the cry had dulled it. He couldn't blame anybody for refusing to see the menace. The crops were luxuriant on every hand, and money was pouring into the farmers' pockets. A man would be crazy to pull up and leave. I just started yelling too soon, Mark thought. Hadn't somebody once said a prophet was without honor in his own country. Mark grimaced. But somebody had to squarely face the issue. Somebody had to make plans for a future that assumed the worst. So far, Hodges had failed in his attempt to rechain the river. And Mark could see nothing in his performance that argued any difference.

The loneliness wrapped around him as he started down the street. He had enough money to buy him anything he wanted, except contentment. He guessed money never guaranteed that. Had he been contented at any time in his association with Letty? He had thought about that often and never came to any conclusion. He had tried to see her once more, and she wouldn't come out of the house. He had lost his temper and yelled at her and was ashamed of the entire incident. His marriage was gone. If neither of them did any more about it, it would drag itself to death of its own weary weight.

A passerby spoke to him, and he was so deeply wrapped in his thoughts that he didn't hear him. He hadn't known a lot of happiness in this valley. The only truly happy days was when he was working for Hodges and living with Charley Ross. Amity's coming had changed all that. He meant it as no indictment. It just happened that way.

He wondered how she and Hodges had made out after that scene before Ross's store, and an inner voice asked, why not go find out? Don't you owe her enough interest to find out? He made up his mind abruptly and turned toward Ross's store.

Ross had a greater stock of merchandise than Mark had seen in his store. Ross was keeping up with Brawley's growth.

He frowned at Mark. "Seems like I should know you."

"Cut it out, Charley."

Ross's frown relented. "You're a bad influence. The last time I was with you, you got me drunk."

Mark smiled. "I'd say it was the other way around." He didn't like to think about that evening, for he blamed it for the change in the course of his life. Human nature was like the Colorado River. Put something different like an unusual event in its course, and it forgets its old channel. If Letty hadn't helped him to the hotel, would the following events have happened? He always broke up that thought whenever it occurred to him. A man could pound his head against that wall until it was bloody.

"What's happening at the river, Mark?"

"You probably know more about it than I do."

"You mean through Clell?" Ross shook his head, a heavy, negative gesture. "He's been here a few times. I can't make sense out of what he says. One minute, he's in the clouds with some new plan, and the next he's complaining of the dirty tricks nature and men play on him." He hunted for the exact words he wanted. "He's different."

Mark had no doubt of that. The load Hodges carried would make any man different. Before he could comment, Ross gave him a warning shake of his head.

He turned, and Amity was coming into the store. Was that a flash of gladness at seeing him in her eyes? It was gone too quickly for him to be sure.

"I just got back from the Salton Basin, Mark."

"She goes out there all the time," Ross grumbled. "It's got some kind of hold on her."

She nodded agreement. "Mark, it's so much bigger."

He knew that, though he hadn't seen it again. But he had seen the flood waters pounding at Sharp's.

Her eyes asked a question he couldn't answer. Could Hodges do something about it? He felt a prick of irritation. She was better able to answer it than he was.

He wanted to ease the heaviness of the moment, and he asked, "Why can't we have dinner tonight? All of us?"

There was definite refusal in her face, but Ross accepted before she could say anything. "It'll be a relief from this damned waiting."

Mark's eyes begged her, and she nodded. "I think I'd like that."

The river was the only topic of conversation at dinner. Mark tried to learn Hodges' thinking, and she said shortly, "I don't know. He draws sketches of what he's going to do, but I don't understand them. Then the next time I see him, he's crushed, because something has gone wrong. I'm beginning to hate that river, Mark."

He understood. The river had flowed between her and Hodges for a long time now. In her way, she was fighting it as hard as Hodges was.

He made the dinner last as long as he could. He couldn't call it a happy one, but being with her was compensation enough. Laughter was still in her. When the talk wasn't on the river, it bubbled to the surface as he remembered it.

They came out of the hotel and almost bumped into the Newlins. Letty's eyes blazed at him, and Maud's face was twisted and bitter. Curt looked at him with sad, reproachful eyes.

"Take her back to the store, Charley." He stepped quickly between them and the Newlins. He caught the embarrassment in Amity's face before he faced Letty.

"Are you still trying to hide her?" That was pure hating in Letty's voice.

"Stop it, Letty. I've tried to talk this out with you. But you wouldn't give me a chance."

"I hate you."

Perhaps in her own mind, she had sufficient reason. This wasn't going to be any better than the other times Mark had tried.

Maud tugged on her daughter's arm. "Don't talk to him. He isn't worth it." She pulled her down the street.

Newlin remained a moment. "I wish things were different."

"Does she need anything, Curt?"

"She wouldn't take your money, Mark. Letty's a proud girl."

"Curt," Maud yelled. "Are you coming?"

Newlin gave him an apologetic look before he followed them.

Mark's eyes were sick. This was going to have to be resolved, but a man dreaded the final step.

It was three weeks before Holt returned to town, and Mark had fretted every moment of it. He wasted no time in greetings. "My God, Bill, what's happening out there?"

Holt looked tired, but his greatest weariness was in his eyes. "It's still open, Mark. They've tried one thing after another. Have you heard about Hodges trying to build a pile dam across the river?"

Mark nodded.

"Then you know that didn't work. He tried to build a wooden control gate in the sand north of the crevasse, then divert the river through that. If he could get the river out of the crevasse, he could fill it in, then close his gate. The first site he picked was a quicksand bed, and the foundations sank out of sight. He tried again, and the sand wouldn't hold his structure. Then the railroad sent down a new engineer. He and Hodges decided to go back to the old scheme of building a barrier across the river from the sand island. They got most of the brush mats laid on the river bottom and weighted them down with rocks." He stopped and shrugged. It was more expressive than any words.

"The Gila threw down another flood?"

"This one was a beauty. I listened to the trash in it crash and grind all night long. In the morning, the river flowed thick and straight over the spread-out sand. The weir was gone, and the sand island was swept away by the flood. In the place of the crevasse and diversion ditch was a canyon six hundred feet wide. It carried away tools, supplies, barges, dredges, everything. And it wiped out the two hundred thousand."

"Jesus Christ," Mark breathed. He was afraid to ask how much water was pouring into the valley. "That's it, isn't it, Bill?" It had to be. Hodges was out of money.

There was a wondering quality in Holt's face. "Harriman must be the same kind of stubborn man that Hodges is. He wired that Hodges was to use as much money as necessary to shut off that river. But shut it off."

"And Hodges bounced right off of the ground?"

"He bounced. He came up with a new plan. He knows now that no wood can stand up against the Colorado. It's going to take concrete and steel, bedded down on the solid rock at Hanlon's Heading, well flanked by dikes and protected by trash booms against the debris. Will that do it, Mark?"

"Yes." It would, if another flash flood held off, if Hodges had enough time before next spring's freshet.

"He's going ahead with it, anyway. He's already placed orders for the materials. He even ordered a huge bucket dredge to dig out the old canal." His face was awed. "He doesn't mind spending Harriman's money. The dredge is costing eighty thousand dollars. Harriman's asked me to stay out there. Mark, I'm scared."

That was no admission of weakness. So was Mark. Hodges was now in a race where every minute was valuable.

"Mark, look after things for me here."

It was the least Mark could do. But he felt handcuffs clamping about his wrists.

CHAPTER TWENTY

Waiting is the most horrible pressure a man can bear, and Mark learned there was only one way to get through it—a day at a time. Holt kept him posted about what was happening at the river. Hodges was winning his race. The Gila had relented. It didn't send down a single flood during the winter, and the people so deeply involved with the Colorado began to breathe freer. By April, the large concrete gate above Hanlon's was finished. All that remained to be done was the digging of a short canal to the river. The spring rise had already begun, but it wasn't troublesome yet. If the huge dredge was here, it would be a relatively simple matter to clear the old main canal of sand and divert the river through the new gate. And this one would hold. But the dredge wasn't here. It was packed on flat cars in San Francisco ready to be shipped. The last time Mark had seen Holt, Holt had said, "I'll sleep again, when that dredge is here."

Mark stood on a street corner, talking to Ross. He shook his head in answer to Ross's question. "The dredge should be here by now, Charley. They promised it by the middle of April, and it's past that now. We'll have to wait until Bill gets back to know."

He was tired spiritually and physically. Once the river was chained, he thought he would leave the valley. This was the place that had given him too many scars, and the only way to forget them was to leave the scene. That always brought its pang, for Amity was still in his thoughts. He hadn't seen her since that unfortunate night. Even if she would permit it, he wouldn't risk causing her that kind of embarrassment again.

He started to say something, and the ground under his feet trembled. His eyes must be going bad, for it looked as though the buildings across the street trembled. And in the distance was a heavy rumbling noise like the sound of a distant freight train.

Ross identified it immediately. "Earthquake," he yelled and plunged for the middle of the street.

Mark rushed after him. At least, they'd have a better chance of escaping falling walls out here.

People rushed into the street, their faces strained, as they called fearful questions back and forth to one another. The brick façade of Arnold's store peeled off and crashed, puffing up a cloud of dust. Several panes of glass shattered, a lesser tinkling noise in the cacophony of heavier sound.

Mark felt several tremors run through the earth under his feet, and a small crack opened up in the street. But it wasn't a bad earthquake; it had caused some minor damage and a great deal of fear. But the major shock of the earth movement wasn't centered here. The length of California set on one gigantic fault, and he thought that some-place in the state had received fearful damage.

The fear melted as the earth remained stable, and each person had to tell his reaction to the quake. Reports filtered in from nearby farms. Thousands of tons of sand had slid into distribution canals, and men grumbled at the task of digging them out, but relief was open on their faces that it hadn't been worse.

Mark wondered if Hodges' new concrete gate had suffered any damage. He would have to wait to find out.

They got the news in a couple of days. San Francisco was completely destroyed. Then correcting information followed. Some of the city still stood, but it had suffered unbelievable wounds. And the loss of life had been heavy. Mark was tempted to ride out to the river. Then he thought he had better wait until Holt came in.

He saw him riding toward town at the end of the week, and the dejection in Holt's slumped figure told him whatever had happened out there had been bad.

He ran forward to meet him, and Holt shook his head. His face and voice were equally dull. "It's finished, Mark. Hodges got a telegram from Harriman. The dredge was buried under tons of rubble. It will take at least six months to repair it."

Mark felt an insane desire to rave and swear. Without the dredge, Hodges' new gate was useless.

"I saw Harriman's wire. He's putting his entire time and fortune to the rescue of San Francisco. He ended it by saying, 'this act of God destroys your hopes. Advise you fight on as best you can.'"

They looked at each other, and both of them knew. There was nothing left to fight with.

"Mark, I guess this decides it. It makes Hodges the unluckiest man in the world."

"Is the river rising?"

"It's rising. You can see it hour by hour."

Mark felt cruel pressure as though giant hands were squeezing his chest. The valley was at the mercy of a mad, rampaging river.

"He got another telegram, too. The Mexican government wired approval for his gate design."

Mark clenched his fists. The spot where that gate was to have gone had been washed away weeks ago.

His laughter was a harsh, metallic sound, and Holt stared at him. Mark couldn't stop his laughter long enough to explain that he wasn't crazy. If he didn't laugh, he would cry.

The river rose through the remainder of April and filled the Mexican countryside. Hundreds of farmers fled before it. The yellow water crept over the flat delta land, gulping awesome amounts of land. Reports said that Volcano Lake was overflowing and spreading toward the north. There was no longer a river out there; it was an ocean. Once that vast body of water reached the downward slope at the border, all of Imperial Valley lay helpless before it.

Mark haunted the New River and Alamo barrancas. The flood waters rose hourly. Eleven thousand Imperial farmers were caught between the two streams that sliced through the desert soil. Mark knew that Hodges was fighting the river, trying to turn it back with every trick at his command. But he might as well have tried to turn back a gale with his hands.

May burned into June, and the spring freshet topped the Colorado channel with seventy thousand second-feet. The Delta was completely inundated. And the crest of the spring rise was still six weeks away. The people who knew were saying the water would double in volume before the end of the rise. If New River and Alamo couldn't carry the excess water away to the Salton Basin, the valley was lost.

And still Mark could convince few people that actual danger existed. The only thing that really occupied people was the ripening cantaloupe crop. Men remembered the enormous amount of money it had put into their pockets last spring. Walk away and leave that money? Did Mark think they were crazy?

New River wound north out of Mexico from Volcano Lake through the border towns of Mexicali and Calexico, then cut across the valley to the Salton. At the upper end, New River and the Alamo converged upon a narrow neck of land where Brawley stood. Mark believed that narrow neck was under the most immediate menace. Already, a new highway bridge across New River to West Mesa settlement had been ripped out. The emergency had been met with a flatboat ferry and an aerial tramway of cables and basket that shuttled back and forth high above the flood. They laughed and joked, and they believed that the Colorado had already thrown her worst at them.

At the end of a week, Mark gave up trying to warn the people. He guessed he didn't have the convincing appearance of a Paul Revere. He didn't know Amity was near until she touched his arm.

"Mark, you've done all you can."

Her face looked truly concerned, but he had no time to put a personal connotation on it. "But not enough, Amity. They can't see what it'll be like, when twice, three times the amount of water comes down. The sandy banks of the barrancas can't stand against it. Do you remember I once told you quick water cuts like a knife?"

She nodded, and her eyes never left his face.

"Every bend in these crooked barrancas is going to put a spin on that racing water. Those whirlpools will undercut the protruding banks and topple them. We're going to lose whole farms before this is through."

She wasn't scoffing or disinterested. Every word he said was vital to her.

"And when the Salton Sink fills up, it'll come down on us from the north. We'll be caught between two blades."

She shivered. "That sea frightens me, Mark."

"It would frighten any sane person, Amity. I haven't seen it for almost a week. I want to look at it." It wouldn't do any good, but he had to do something to keep him occupied.

"Take me with you, Mark."

He nodded abruptly. Both of them needed the solace of companionship.

He drove the runabout to where New River poured into the Salton Basin. The muddy water raced down the last stretch of this sloping desert country, fanning out and building a delta of its own. The heavy sand had already piled up a rounded bulge of new land, and the river rode on top of it, branching off into a dozen streams before it raced to the sea.

Mark watched the largest stream. It humped in a wave over some obstruction and fell on the other side in a miniature waterfall.

How well he remembered his first description of the Colorado to Amity. "Throw as much as a single pebble into it, and you might change the face of geography." Was this the pebble?

He saw what was causing the obstruction, a small log caught in the current and plowed under and held. The water rising over it had gouged a hole on its farther side, making the miniature waterfall. There was no doubt about it. The fall had grown in the few moments he had been watching it.

He had the instinctive fear that this log was the start of everything. If the log would only wash away, maybe the river would smooth out again. He looked about for something to dislodge it, but he could find nothing long enough to even begin to reach it.

"What is it, Mark?"

Before he could answer her, the log sprang upward and was washed down the current. He wanted to shout his relief. "Nothing, Amity. A fantasy I was building in my head."

But it wasn't a fantasy, and it wasn't in his head. It was real and before him. The river hadn't smoothed out. The fall was increasing in height and spreading across the channel. The smaller streams were joining in and increasing the volume of the falling water. The basin below the crest was a boiling cauldron, and the noise had grown until it pounded at a man's ears.

It had to be a fantasy, for no man could credit what he was seeing. The fall was eating its way backward against the current. Inch by inch, the fall was moving its way south, in the opposite direction of the flow of the water.

Amity saw it, too, for she clutched his arm. "Mark, it's moving."

Mark realized what was happening. The wearing action of the water was dissolving the soft mud that made the lip of the fall. As every handful fell away, the crest moved backward. How long could it last? It could last clear across the valley, carving out a gash that would grow to a full-sized canyon. The caving earth would grab off the farms one by one. His own farms would go, though that wasn't paramount in his mind. The town could follow. And over on the Alamo the same situation could happen until a once fertile valley was only a deep gouge in the earth.

He gave her a twisted and terrible grin. "Maybe when they see that, they'll listen to me. I've got to tell them again, Amity."

CHAPTER TWENTY-ONE

A man listened about the cutback, and his face filled with skepticism. Who could believe that a waterfall, twenty feet high, could be approaching through the open desert? But when he saw and heard it, he believed it. People flocked out from Brawley to see this awesome thing, and every face had the stamp of fear on it.

The cutback was moving up New River faster than a mile a day. Less than five miles separated it from Brawley. It sounded like distant thunder, and people slept uneasily because of its noise. In less than a week, it would have to stop, or Brawley would be wiped out.

Mark swore and raved. People should be thinking of danger to themselves, and they weren't. They were thinking of saving the cantaloupe crop before it was snatched from them. Farmers gathered their burlap sacks and greased their wagons, for the crop was almost ripe. In the middle of June, the harvest began. Long lines of cantaloupe wagons rattled over the desert toward the railroad. Crate after crate slid along the handling line in the packing sheds. Expert hands packed the tissue-wrapped fruit. The packed boxes were shoved along to the freight cars, waiting in the shade of canopies outside. Great cakes of ice skidded along the runways from the ice plant to be dumped down the hatches. The roar of the approaching cutback drowned out the sound of the switching engines as they pulled out loaded cars onto the siding and replaced them with empties under the sheds. Out by the water tank a big Mallet engine waited for the next long fruit express to be made up. Men worked until they dropped, for the cantaloupe crop depended upon the escape of the trains from Brawley. Only one exit was left, the Southern Pacific bridge at Alamorio going north. This crossing over the Alamo was the only link with the outside world.

The smaller barranca was in flood, too, and what Mark had feared was happening. A cutback was moving southward along it, bearing down on the lone railroad bridge. The bridge, with its wooden piling, could not stand. When it went, whatever part of the crop was unshipped was lost.

So men, women, and children worked. Time lost all meaning, as they tore ripe and green fruit from the vines. They put them in sacks slung over their backs, in hand carts and wagons. They worked until they couldn't take another step, then cut their resting time until it wasn't nearly sufficient. They stuffed sandwiches down and gulped coffee in the fields, and when the sun was gone, the light of lanterns danced like myriads of fireflies. They were winning their battle against time, but they were losing far more, for they didn't give a thought to their homes and personal possessions.

Mark and Charley Ross had been up all night but not picking cantaloupes. They had begged the people to move inland, to take what they could carry and get out. They had begged until they were hoarse and never swerved a picker.

As the sun came up, Mark and Ross were red-eyed and stumbling with fatigue. "My God," Ross said. "They didn't even listen to us."

Mark thought grimly, they'll listen to the cutback before long. At this distance, the barranca wasn't visible below the level of the plain. But it was marked by the great pillar of dust and spray that hung over it. The sound was the crashing of artillery barrages. Those heavy, crashing booms were pieces of the lip letting go and dropping into the canyon. Yesterday, Mark had seen pieces of earth let go that weighed tons.

"Charley, Newlin's farm is only a few miles out of town. It's right in the path of the cutback. Have you seen them lately?"

Ross's face paled. "No, but they can't be there now, Mark, can they?"

"I don't know." The rest of the cantaloupe pickers were. Mark had no reason to suppose Newlin would be any different. "But I've got to find out."

He refused Ross's offer of help and ran to the livery stable. If necessary, he would manhandle the Newlins away from that barranca's edge.

He saw Newlin at the far end of the field, moving bent over through the vines. Newlin was this side of the house, and the crashing booms and the spray marked the cutback as being just a little beyond it.

He got Newlin's attention and waved him to him. Newlin reluctantly laid down his picking sack and came forward. Mark ran to the brink of the falls. Each time he saw it it was a new shock. It grew in destructive powers so rapidly. It was now a chasm a hundred feet deep and fully five hundred feet wide from rim to rim. In the bottom, a maelstrom of water spun crazily, laden with debris of every description. He saw bits of houses, pieces of wooden bridges, brush and trees, and the bodies of cattle and pigs.

Newlin joined Mark and stared with him into that abyss. Only the same awe wasn't on his face. He looked almost apologetic as he glanced at Mark. "Guess I've seen it too much. She's slicing off a hell of a lot of my land though."

It wouldn't do any good to yell and swear at him. He didn't feel the danger because he simply didn't understand it. Mark forced his voice calm. "Where's Letty and Maud?"

"In the house." Newlin guessed at what Mark was going to say. "No danger to them. It'll cut pretty close to the house, but it won't take it."

Mark's teeth were on edge. "You're risking all your furniture, everything you own in that house to pick a few more cantaloupes."

Newlin looked injured. "That's my cash crop. I need it. I was only picking the ones closest to the edge. It's not going to take the house."

Mark seized him around the waist and flung him backward. He made it rough. It had to be to get Newlin over the great crack that suddenly developed in the earth. It first showed a couple of feet behind them, and now the piece of earth from crack to brink was shuddering as it slowly sank. It picked up momentum and then it was out of sight. Mark's ears were pounded by the deep boom that followed, and a gust of dust mixed with spray puffed up out of the chasm. Mark heard the groaning of the debris as it rolled and cracked again. That was made by the tremendous wave action the dropping piece of earth caused.

Newlin gulped, and his face was pale. "I didn't see that coming." He took several more backward steps, and his legs weren't steady.

"Now will you get those women out?"

Newlin licked his lips, and fear had finally entered his eyes. "Guess I'd better." He turned and surprised Mark with the speed with which he moved.

Maud was out in front of the house, and Newlin yelled, "Get Letty out. The ground's falling into the river. Don't try to save anything." He believed now, and it had a terrible urgency.

Maud's eyes blazed at Mark. "Letty saw him here. She won't come out."

Mark's words were drowned by another boom. An even bigger chunk of land dropped out of sight, and he could see cracks radiating toward the house. He was losing time, arguing with Maud. He would have to go in and drag Letty out.

Another deep roar came just as he reached the house. The cutback seemed to be speeding up. He had trouble opening the door. The land seemed to have settled enough to warp the door against its frame. He slammed his shoulder against it and broke it open. Only one inside door was closed.

"Letty, come out here." Mark tried the knob, and it was locked. "Letty, damn it. The house is going."

"Go away," she screamed. "I swore I'd never talk to you again."

He threw a shoulder against the door, but he didn't have enough momentum. He backed off for several feet for a harder run, and the house groaned and creaked, momentarily stopping his breathing. He tried to take a step, and the floor tilted beneath him, spilling him from his feet. He rolled into a far wall, and Letty's screaming was now an undiminishing burst of sound.

He looked at that closed door. Even if the tilting hadn't frozen it shut, he had no way to force it open. He would be lucky to make it back to the outer door.

He tried to shut his ears to the screaming. The house groaned in constant torture, as he clawed his way up the increasing tilt of the floor. He reached the threshold and dragged himself over it. He stood, balancing himself between the jambs, then made a frantic leap. He landed on the crumbling ledge, and his feet slipped in the disintegrating earth. He clawed and kicked his way upward, using strength he didn't know he had. Later, he was to find his nails torn and bleeding. He heaved himself over the last few inches, and the earth dropped rapidly where he had just been. He rolled and scrambled, trying to give himself a greater margin of safety. When he turned his head, the house was out of sight. He winced at the following crash. Above that noise, he thought he heard screaming, screaming that tore out his guts.

Maud struggled in Newlin's arms, trying to run forward. "You can't," Newlin yelled over and over. "Nobody can do anything."

Mark put his feet under him and joined them. His body had never known such a pounding as he had given it in those few seconds.

"I tried. I couldn't—" His voice died.

Maud looked at him, and a face could hold no more hating. "You didn't want to save her. You didn't—"

Newlin's eyes were shocked, as he clamped a hand over her mouth.

"She doesn't mean that. She's out of her head with grief."

She meant it, Mark thought drearily. In a way, he was responsible, for one event had led to another.

"She needs attention. I gotta get her to town."

"Take my horse, Curt."

Newlin's eyes were sick, but he kept his voice surprisingly gentle. "She wouldn't take nothing from you now."

Mark knew he was right. "If you need any money—"

Newlin shook his head again. That belonged to Mark, too.

Mark turned abruptly away from them. Everything they had was gone. Should he feel more grief, or was reaction dulling him to it? For a short while, he had been a member of this family. It must have been a tenuous bond for its breaking to leave no more wound than this.

CHAPTER TWENTY-TWO

Ross was waiting for him when he returned to Brawley. He was a wise man. He looked at Mark's eyes and didn't ask questions.

But Mark had to get this out, and maybe in the telling of it he would find his ease. "Newlin lost at least half of his farm. The house was on it. Letty was inside."

The "ah" was jolted out of Ross. His eyes widened, then his face resumed its normal expression. He wouldn't pry at Mark.

Mark shook his head, and let the talk stop. He hadn't fully assayed his responsibility in this. Someday, he might be able to evaluate it fully. Right now, he couldn't bear to think about it.

"What do we do now, Mark?" Ross grinned apologetically. "It hardly seems fitting to go ahead tending a store."

Mark nodded his understanding. "Wherever a pair of hands are needed, Charley."

They spent four brutal days, helping wherever they could. Very little of their effort was successful. They worked shoulder to shoulder with farmers, laying down rip-raps of brush, hoping it would stop the cutting action of the water. Most of the work was wasted, for the small mesquite trees and arrow-weed stalks were thrown aside by the water the minute they were laid in place. They watched farm after farm fall away. Wherever the channel bent, the water struck sideways at the projecting bank of soil, and the land broke off and fell in. Any man whose farm was on a point lost it, or at least a sizable portion of it. Brawley suffered, too, though the destruction wasn't as great as had been feared. The town lost a few buildings, but the majority of it was intact, perched precariously on the barranca's edge. When people were convinced that a miracle had happened, that most of their town had been saved, they came back to the empty buildings. Mark heard the laughter of relief in their voices. In a few hours, living would be back to as nearly normal as it could be. But the telling of this would last as long as man's memory.

"You're leaving, aren't you, Mark?"

Mark glanced at him in surprise, and Ross grinned faintly. "It shows in your face."

"I'm thinking of that cutback." It had passed beyond Brawley, but its menace still remained. When it reached Sharp's gate, it would destroy it, and the last possible control of the river would be gone.

"You're going to try to stop it?"

"I don't know what I'm going to do, Charley, but I've got to do something."

"I knew it. I already told Amity I was going with you."

Mark glanced at him with a curious alertness. "What did she say?"

"Nothing. Except be careful."

Mark wondered why her reaction should have come as a surprise to him. But most women would have taken an opposite stand. "Can you leave now?"

"I'm ready."

They rode south to Imperial. A few miles outside of town, they ran into water, a vast sheet of water that covered the land as far as the eye could see. The last two miles were hazardous, and the horses moved a cautious step at a time, fearful of stepping into an invisible hole or ditch.

Mark fretted about all this water. Where had it come from? There had to be a serious break in one of the levees—or the Colorado had overwhelmed Sharp's gate and was inundating the land.

They stopped before Ross's old building in Imperial. Stores were flooded, and houses were isolated in their yards. Adobe buildings were slowly melting away on their foundations.

The people had made an attempt to curb the creeping waters. Houses and stores stood behind their bulwarks of sandbags and brush. Every type of conceivable sack had been filled with sand. Seed, grain, flour, and sugar sacks were piled against the onslaught, and Mark saw sacks made of sheets, curtains, pillowcases and even old clothes. Men moved with the dragging step of utter weariness, and their eyes were hollow from the strain of vigil. For there was no rest. Where a bulwark was strengthened here, it crumbled there, and men had to rush more sacks to the constant threat.

Ross looked at his old building. Water lapped at the second step, but as yet it hadn't entered the store. "And I can remember praying for water."

Mark smiled faintly and stepped into the building. Two great piles of sugar and flour took up a lot of the floor.

The new store owner looked at them sadly. "I dumped them out for the sacks. It's no good now, but I just kinda hated to throw it out."

Mark nodded in sympathy. "Where did this water come from?"

"The main irrigation canal at El Centro broke wide open. Calexico and Mexicali are in worse shape than we are. Everybody's getting out, carrying what they can. There's been a string of wagons through here every day."

He managed a mirthless grin. "We're sitting in a lake. The alkali won't let the water soak it. And more keeps coming. Damned if I think it'll ever stop."

He picked up a bottle from the counter. "Want a drink?"

Mark shook his head.

"That's about all there is to do. Wait and drink.

One keeps the other from driving a man crazy. If this doesn't break up pretty soon, I guess we're all lost."

Mark's eyes widened. It was there all the time, and he hadn't seen it. "Have you any dynamite?"

The man looked at him as though he was crazy. "Maybe a couple of boxes."

Ross had the same expression, and it deepened as they lashed the boxes behind the saddle.

"Charley, when he said break up, it hit me. I'm going to dynamite those falls. If I can hurry it south, we might be able to save Calexico and Mexicali."

Ross shook his head. "I didn't see you take a drink."

"Doesn't that cutback leave a deep, wide canyon? If I can hurry it through the towns before they go under, wouldn't all the flood waters pour into that canyon?"

"You know more about it than I do. I suppose I'll be able to help you with it? I thought so. I don't see how I can stay so goddamned lucky."

They rode south through the flooded land. It gave a man a queer, insecure feeling to see water wherever he looked. No longer was the Colorado chuckling slyly; it laughed out loud in insensate merriment.

New River barranca cut through the edge of both Calexico and Mexicali, and the people of the twin towns had worked frantically to save them. They had built a sandbag levee along New River, but that levee wasn't going to be enough to save the towns. The water outside it rose steadily, and the sandbags leaked a hundred muddy pencil streams.

Already, the water outside the sandbags was ten feet deep, and its pressure was working on the levee's footing. If the pressure continued, it would throw that bulwark aside.

He called for volunteers, and half of the town of Calexico responded. He told them of the danger and didn't see a man flinch. Danger! They had been living with it for weeks.

He turned to begin his preparations, and a light hand touched his arm. "Señor, you would want me, wouldn't you?"

"Tomás." Mark's face shone with genuine pleasure. "You know I want you. But your job?"

"The farm is under water. I was on my way back to my village. They needed help here." He shrugged expressively. "So I stayed."

Mark clapped him on the shoulder. "We chained the wild bull before. We'll do it again."

"I hope so, señor." There wasn't conviction in Tomás' voice.

The cutback had reached a point sixteen miles above Calexico. Mark had all the dynamite in the twin towns brought to the falls and sent additional men to El Centro for more. He looked at the terrifying force of the cutback, and a million doubts assailed him.

Ross's eyes were riveted to the falls. "And you're going to hurry it up by blasting the crest of it? I'd want to kill that damned thing, not give it more life."

"I'll try to kill it after it passes the towns, Charley. Right now, we need the canyon it makes. Maybe it'll die in Volcano Lake or in the Mexican swamps."

"Will you tell me how you're going to get dynamite under that falls?"

"I'll drift down in a boat until I'm right above the brink. Then I'll let down a box of dynamite with a long, lighted fuse."

Ross stared in horror. "What's to keep you from drifting on over? You can't row against that current."

"There'll be a long rope on that boat. That's why I need so many men—to hang onto it. As soon as I signal, I'm hoping they'll drag me back quick."

Ross mournfully shook his head. "I'm crazy. But I'm going with you."

Tomás was standing near enough to overhear, and Mark saw the sorrow touch his face. "No, Charley. Tomás is going. We've worked together before."

The two faces were a comparison. Tomás' had a kind of joy; Ross's had a mixture of anger and relief.

Mark climbed into the boat and looked up at Ross. "You just see that you hang onto this rope."

Slowly, the boat was played downstream at the end of the long rope. Tomás' face looked serene enough, but he gripped the gunwales with a force that made his knuckles stand out. Mark knew that strain, the strain that racked a man physically and emotionally.

The water slapped at the stern, trying to speed the boat. Mark looked back just once at the men holding onto the rope. If they let go, or the strain proved too great, Mark and Tomás would be swept over the falls.

Talk was impossible as they neared the brink. The roar was a physical force, and mist made a thick, blinding curtain. The rope was let out a few inches at a time, then snubbed, and the jerks snapped Mark's head backward and forward. Now it took the finest of judgment. If the boat was let out too far, it would overbalance and slide over the falls. And no man would survive that drop.

The boat stopped its forward progress, and the taut rope hummed. The boat picked up side motion, swinging back and forth like a pendulum. Mark fused a box of dynamite, clambered to the bow, and looked over into the abyss. The mist and lashing waters were a churning, twisting hell. He broke his fixed, fascinated gaze. If a man looked too long, he felt a power pulling at him.

He tied a rope about the dynamite, lighted the

fuse, and lowered it. He waved for Tomás to jerk on the boat's rope as the prearranged signal to drag them back. He breathed again when he felt the boat's movement in the reverse direction. He hoped the dynamite had stuck at the bottom of the falls and not carried away. But there was no dynamite report. By the time the boat was pulled back to the bank, he knew the dynamite wasn't going off. Something had happened. Maybe the water had extinguished the fuse.

He grimaced and picked up another box of dynamite.

Ross grabbed his arm. "Mark, you're not going out there again?" His hand dropped away. He knew he was.

They went through the torturous trip all over, but Mark thought both of them were less tense. Repetition had a way of dulling danger's teeth. He wrapped the fuse well in rags, shortened it, then lowered the box. The dynamite blast came before they had been pulled twenty-five yards. Muddy water and solid chunks of earth showered them, and when the mist and smoke lessened, a huge, crescent-shaped bite had been chewed out of the brink. The edge crumbled into the canyon for a long time after the shot. The shot had hastened the cutting action of the water.

All the rest of the day Mark and Tomás placed dynamite shots under the brink of the falls. By nightfall he estimated he had doubled the speed of the cutback. He staggered ashore and dropped. Somebody offered him food and coffee, and he shook his head. He only wanted to lie here for a few eternities.

He was drugged with weariness in the morning. He winced as he sat up. He ached in every muscle. The pounding of the boat, and the strain of anxious hours were demanding their price.

Ross was still asleep, and Mark decided against waking him. He looked toward the canal's edge and recognized the strained attitude of the line of men. They were playing out the rope. Somebody was being lowered to the brink's edge.

He jumped to his feet and ran toward them. Tomás was in the boat, almost to the falls, and Mark shouted, "Bring him back."

One of the men panted, "He wanted to go. He said more than one man should fight the river. He'll be all right. He wanted you to rest. He watched you all day yesterday. He knows how to do it."

The boat was halted on the brink. A rent in the mist appeared, and Mark saw Tomás plainly. "Tomás," he yelled.

Tomás couldn't possibly hear him, but he looked around as though he did. He raised an arm in a wave, then bent back to his work. He played out the rope on the dynamite from the bow.

Mark had a sudden premonition of impending tragedy. "Pull him back!" One man should never have gone out there alone, and he cursed himself for oversleeping.

The boat came back with maddening slowness. It was only feet from the edge of the falls when the blast came. Mark's groan was an unconscious sound jerked from him. He couldn't see for the dense cloud of spray and earth, but he knew the boat had been too close.

"Pull!" His face and voice weren't sufficient vehicles for his frenzy. He grabbed the rope and hauled on it, and it came with no resistance. A piece of the stern was still fastened to it; the rest was gone.

He ran along the barranca like a wild man. He passed the falls, and his lungs ached with screaming Tomás' name. A few shattered boards bobbed in the whirlpool below the falls. He stared until his eyes ached, and nothing else appeared. He plodded miles down the newly formed canyon's edge, and it was futile.

Ross met him coming back. "It's no use, Mark."

"No," Mark answered dully. "He was a brave man. He always feared the river." He put a last look on the rushing waters, remembering the loneliness in Tomás' eyes since Lupita had gone. He doubted that going on had made much difference to Tomás.

The dynamiting forced the cutback between the twin towns a week early, and it came none too soon. A strong south wind lashed the water over the dikes, and the sandbags leaked in too many places to be controlled. The cutback drove its wide canyon through the western corner of Calexico and Mexicali, shearing away land beneath stores, warehouses, and dwellings. But the flood waters drained into it, and what was left of the towns was saved. By night, the land was drying, and objects that had been inundated for days came into view.

The canyon refused to end in the Mexican swamps. It crossed the border, a hundred feet deep, and slashed its way across Volcano Lake. Mark had a couple of weeks at the most. Then Sharp's gate would go, and the cutback would reach the main Colorado with no hope of controlling it. It could devour Yuma and gulp the Laguna dam. When that happened, all Southwest irrigation stopped.

More dynamiting would only give it additional speed. It had to be divided, making it shear into smaller streams. Then the smaller streams might be able to be killed one at a time.

Mark hired a gang of Indian and Mexican laborers and set them to building brush weirs. He had a barge towed in from the river and planted the brush mats with stakes in the cutback's path.

The waterfall split cleanly in two around the obstruction, the halves setting off at right angles to each other. He attacked the northern half and saw it die against his brush weirs.

The southern half was a devil. It sucked up load after load of brush. But the work was narrowing it. Yet it was still a powerful force when it reached the rocky point of Black Butte, jutting out into the lake.

He made his final stand there. He worked the laborers day and night, building a series of weirs in a rough semicircle below the point, hoping to pocket the cutback.

He watched it approaching his weirs. "If this doesn't work, Charley, I'm finished."

Their eyes were riveted on the narrowed falls. Ross gripped his arm, and Mark wasn't aware of it.

The cutback struck the weirs and broke into a dozen smaller falls. The main body of the current swerved to the west and turned back under Black Butte's rocky shore. The water shoaled to a few inches, and the remaining whirlpool seemed lifeless after the mighty force of the preceding one.

"It's dying, Mark. You've killed it." Ross realized he didn't have to yell. The roar of the falls was gone. The desert had fallen back into its brooding silence.

Yes, it was dead. Mark had stomped the life out of it here. It had slashed a destructive path through seventy miles of the rich valley. Its bill was staggering in destroyed property and hopes. And there was greater cost. There was Letty and Tomás.

CHAPTER TWENTY-THREE

The report reached Brawley from the south. The cutback was dead. Mark Addison had whipped it on the Mexican side. Men stood on corners and talked about the wonder of it, and the belief they had once had in Hodges was gone. Not a few men said openly that if Addison had been in charge all along, none of this disaster would have happened.

Holt found Amity in Ross's store. Her eyes glowed as she asked, "Have you heard about the cutback, Bill?"

"I heard. It only proves my contention. If any man can whip the Colorado, it's Mark." He waited for her reaction.

"Yes." It was a simple word, but it told him everything.

He seized her hands. "E. P. Harriman is in town. He wants to make another attempt to stop the river. Would you tell him what you just said to me?"

She briefly closed her eyes as though she felt pain. But they were clear when she looked at him again. "Yes."

Holt squeezed her hands before he released them. He had shoved her into a rough spot.

Three men were in the hotel room when Amity

and Holt entered it. Holt introduced them, and if Harriman was surprised to see a woman here, it didn't show. The other two were Engle and Brimhall, Southern Pacific engineers. They were capable-looking men with weather-beaten faces, and sun-squint lines fanning out from the corners of their eyes. Both of them looked unhappy, as though a problem, too great to handle, rode their shoulders.

"She's no stranger to this," Holt said. "I think she knows Clell Hodges as well as anybody could."

Harriman searched her face and didn't comment on what he found there.

"A lot of people still believe in him," Brimhall said.

Amity glanced at him, and her lips moved in a sad, little smile, but she remained silent.

Harriman looked at her with penetrating eyes. "If the railroad furnishes everything that's needed, is Hodges the man to direct it?"

There was no hesitation in her. "No."

Harriman's eyes sharpened. "Do you have a recommendation in mind?"

"Mark Addison."

Harriman glanced at Holt. "Why?"

Amity fortified herself with a deep breath. "Because he knows that river better than any other man. And he fears it."

"Ah," Harriman murmured. He was silent for a

256

long moment, drawing aimless lines on a piece of paper. "We just came from Yuma. The late summer rise is beyond all records. The river gauge there shows a flow of ninety-six thousand cubic feet per second. That means eight billion cubic feet of water racing down New River and Alamo barrancas. The Salton Basin is spreading with a rush where once it crept. This disaster is becoming known countrywide. Some of the Los Angeles papers are headlining that the entire coastline might be lost."

She nodded. She knew all this, except the figures.

"We're concerned over our mainline tracks running east. The roadbed has already been moved a half-dozen times, and the trains still crawl through water for miles. Do you still say Addison can handle the responsibility?"

"Yes."

"Where is he now?"

Holt interrupted. "The last we heard he was in the twin border towns. I told you about him killing the cutback?"

Harriman nodded. Something was on his mind, and he had trouble putting it into words. He looked squarely at Amity. "How can you be sure about Addison and Hodges?"

Her face paled, but her head was held high. "Because I am engaged to Clell."

Harriman's surprise showed on his face. He

nodded imperceptibly as though some last doubt was satisfied.

He turned his head toward Holt. "Can you find Addison?"

Holt's eyes touched Amity's face. "We can find him."

"Then get him out to the river as fast as you can. Tell him to send in a list of what he wants. I'll back every demand."

He advanced toward Amity and held out his hand. "Thank you, Miss Ross."

She walked through the doorway ahead of Holt then faced him. "Did you expect me to go with you, Bill?"

"Yes. As my witness to what Harriman said. Mark might not believe my story by itself."

"Bill, please don't say anything about my part in the talk."

He didn't know why, but she had her reasons. "If you want it that way, Amity."

They found Mark in El Centro on his way back to Brawley. Several nights' sleep hadn't erased the fatigue lines in his face. His look grew more incredulous as he listened to Holt's account. "You're crazy, Bill."

"Ask Amity. She heard it."

She nodded quickly. "Mr. Harriman wants you. He will not advance any more money to Clell. I'm riding to the river with you."

He could read nothing in her face. Why was she

going? He wished she wouldn't stay for the confrontation with Hodges was going to be difficult enough.

They rode through a country that had been scarred by the river. There was little talk for each person was locked in their own thoughts. Mark wanted to run from the coming job.

Amity gasped when she saw the enormous amount of water flowing through Hodges' Mexican cut. One man or ten thousand seemed such a puny force to throw against it.

Mark looked at it for so long that Amity worried about him. "Mark."

His face was sober. "It's been months since I've seen it. I can't believe it's widened this much. The mouth of the intake is a good twelve hundred feet wide now. And it started from such a few feet."

Her eyes were on his face, and he thought, she can read me. "You're right, Amity. I'm scared."

"Can you do it?"

He gave it sober reflection, and his attempt at a grin was nearer a grimace. "Ask me in a few months."

He wanted to add more, but Hodges had seen them and was hurrying toward them. He scowled at Mark, his face only smoothing out when he looked at Amity. "Amity, what are you doing here?"

"I came out to see you, Clell."

That put no joy in him, for he flashed Mark a suspicious glance. "Everything's been against me," he said petulantly. "The river sweeps away my brush weirs before I hardly get them laid. And it yanks out my pilings as fast as I put them down."

His eyes were dull with fatigue, and Mark thought, he has courage. How many men could have taken the beating the river had handed him and still be on their feet? He felt a pity for what he had to do. He merely had to kick the heart out of a man.

A gleam started in Hodges' eyes. "But I thought of a new approach last night. This time I'll whip it for sure."

"There won't be another time, Clell." Mark put it as gently as he could.

Hodges had the stupid look of a man wrestling with something beyond his capacity. Mark expected Amity to move to him, lending her nearness to his support. But she stood where she was, and that looked like pain in her eyes.

"What do you mean?" Hodges' eyes swung from Mark to Amity.

"Harriman is taking you off of the job."

A club blow couldn't have stunned him more. He wrestled with the words until he understood them, then his face turned ugly. "I see it now. While I was out here, trying to save the valley, you undercut me with Harriman. You talked your way into my job. If you'd followed my orders and built the gate at Hanlon's right in the first place, none of this would have happened."

The pain was gone from Amity's face, and her eyes were sharp and cold. "Stop it, Clell. He built the gate right. You refused to take advantage of it."

"He withheld information from me. If he had told me about those flashboards—"

The set of her face was colder. "He told you about them. Have you forgotten? I was there when Mark asked why you didn't simply remove them to let in more water."

Hodges blinked, and for a moment was speechless. "He never told me about them. I told him so that day."

Her face was tired now. "And you lied, Clell. I saw it in your eyes."

Mark stepped in. "This isn't doing anybody any good, Clell. Harriman ordered it. And it's his money."

Hodges' face alternately paled and flushed, then his laugh was low and nasty. "Good. I'll enjoy seeing you fall flat on your face. Come on, Amity."

Her voice was rock-steady. "I'm not going, Clell."

That was the hardest blow of all for him to take. He made a half-dozen attempts at speech, and no sound came. She never wavered before the pleading in his eyes, and he turned and plunged away. He stumbled as he moved like a man walking blind.

"He couldn't change." She shook her head sorrowfully.

"He had two natures to whip, Amity. His, and this one. With a little luck he might have won. Remember, he saw this dream first." He wasn't sure, but her eyes may have been a little misty.

"Mark, I said before you were a more charitable man than he was."

He thought he could have taken her into his arms, but Holt was approaching them.

Holt's eyes were on Hodges' retreating figure. "Bad, huh?"

"Bad enough. Bill, take her back to Brawley." He stilled the protest forming in her face. "We'll be out here for weeks, Amity. I only hope there's enough time before the Gila throws its winter floods at us." He pulled a piece of paper and a pencil from his pocket. "Take this partial list back to Harriman." He scribbled rapidly as he talked. "I'll need dredges, river steamers, barges, steam shovels, and pile drivers. And every flatcar the railroad can furnish. I want a track built from Yuma, and then I want rock. I want all the rock in the country. And I'll need men by the thousands."

"You're planning on dumping rock into the river?"

"Hodges proved piles won't hold. I'll saturate it with rock."

"But they'll keep on sinking in the soft bottom."

"I'll dump them in until we find solid footing." He laughed shakily. "I believe it will work, Bill. Something has to chain the wild bull and I believe my rock dams will do it. And God help us if I'm wrong."

He turned to Amity. "It'll be weeks before I see you. Will you wait for me?"

The shining in her eyes was all the answer he needed. "It will work, Mark! It will work, and I'll be waiting!"

Center Point Large Print
600 Brooks Road / PO Box 1
Thorndike ME 04986-0001 USA

(207) 568-3717

US & Canada:
1 800 929-9108
www.centerpointlargeprint.com